POINT GUARD

ATOPON BOOKS

Atopon Books
907 15th Street
Santa Monica, California 90403
United States

Publisher's Cataloging-in-Publication data

Names: Mattessich, Stefan, author.
Title: Point Guard / Stefan Mattessich.
Description: Santa Monica, CA: Atopon Books, 2023.
Identifiers: LCCN 2022946428 | ISBN: 978-1-64713-992-6 (paperback)
Subjects: LCSH Mendocino--Fiction. | California, Northern--Fiction. | Teenagers in literature. | Basketball--Fiction. | Whales--Fiction.
BISAC FICTION / Coming of Age | FICTION / Small Town and Rural | FICTION / Nature and the Environment | FICTION / Sports.
Classification: LCC PS3613.A8329 P58 2023 | DDC 813.6--dc23

Cover: Crushed Paper with a Glowing Center and a Dark Vignette by pamela_d_mcadams / Adobe Stock
Cover Image: "Lighthouse" by Matt Saling on Dribbble
Back Cover: The California gray whale, finback, humpback, and sharp-headed finner from *The Natural History of the Cetaceans and Other Marine Mammals of the Western Coast of North America* (1872) by Charles Melville Scammon / Shutterstock

For
Big Al

WHEN I LOOK BACK on the time I spent growing up in the town of Mendocino, and the events that closed out my adolescent years, what often comes to mind is a moment at the middle school playground with Coach, his son Jordi, and me.

Night had all but set in and the last transparent shimmer of dusk faded slowly from the sky, where a red Mars courted shy proximity with the evening star.

Coach's old Buick town car was angled over the basketball court. The headlights were turned on and the engine was idling. I stood underneath the basket rebounding for Jordi, who suffered under his father's intense judgment. Moths fluttered in the lancing beams. Their agitation matched our mood. Jordi kept getting his shot wrong, and the more he tried, the more he got it wrong. The point past which anything like grace would be possible had been reached.

"Elbow in, straight under the ball, feet lifting," Coach said.

Jordi missed another shot.

"Feet lifting!"

I passed the ball back to him. He lofted it into the night, where it vanished an instant before falling onto the rim, wide of the mark.

"Again," Coach said.

This time he hit nothing but air.

"What did I just say?"

"Lift my feet."

"With your arm under the goddamn ball. Not bent clear out to Kingdom Come like you're doing." Without looking at me, he said, "Give it to him, Woody."

We followed the drill a few more times. Predictably, we got the same bad results. On the last try, the ball bounced back into Jordi's hands. Coach's stare was withering.

"Why is this so hard?" Jordi slumped into the posture of a penitent warding off a blow. Coach saw this, too, and it made him even angrier. "Are you not listening," he said, "or are you just stupid?"

Jordi fought off tears through the silence that followed. I wanted to yell at Coach, force him to stop, but whatever was really going on between them muted my resolve. Jordi rolled the ball in his hands. He tried too hard to concentrate, then dribbled once and pulled up, ramming it defiantly at the basket. The shot banged off the rim. Coach leapt at the ball, took it in one hand, and winged it right back at his son. Jordi recoiled as it glanced off his shoulder and bounded off into the night. I stood shocked for a second before chasing it down. I heard behind me as I ran:

"We're not leaving here until you get it right. I don't care if it takes all night. Do what I goddamn say. . ."

I jogged deeper into darkness, losing the thread of his words. When I caught up to the ball I paused, unsure what to do next. I turned and looked at the two of them. From my vantage point they seemed miniaturized in the headlights' devouring glare, held back in immensity like an emblem of all striving, all harsh insistence, all need for mastery and fear of failure.

That moment, or that emblem, is what I remember. It stays present in the mind when so much of the past has died back, like *the grasses of old summers. Through it a whole world, static now, distant, crystallizes in the imperatives of a father who, too difficult to forget, you could no more stop loving than forgive.*

1

I can't quite catch the feeling of growing up on the Mendocino coast. It's different from what people who don't know might expect. Coming from places where the sea isn't so fixed a presence in their midst, they might appreciate its drama or its beauty, but they tend to idealize it, too. They miss the boredom in restless tides and crumbling rock, in scented breezes and driftwood pushed up against cliff sides.

Locals aren't so lucky. Boredom is often what you feel from day to day. It blocks the inflation of spirit that visitors so eagerly seek. At the same time, I believe it elements the spirit. It affords the ballast you need to bear with the shiver in nature, the apprehension. To those who live by it, the sea is less a comfort than a disquiet, a dread. For all that it rests solidly in its lines of force, commanding respect for its limits and its excesses, it shakes you up, it sways the ground beneath your feet. It lasts the way buried things last.

Mendocino is also a place of edges you come to, surfaces you rub against. Make your heart heavy enough to sink into darkest depths, and it throws you back like a wave. Make your thoughts as light as possible, and they bob against it like cork. People I knew growing up came wanting this peculiar buoyancy. They were good at stopping short of reasons and dreams. Driven into their own margins by some private catastrophe or other, they wanted a truce with desire that would permit them the second chance at life they needed, this time without either illusion or disappointment.

I had a lot of experience with that truce, even though it wasn't mine to have. My mother, Cadie, came to Mendocino after she left my father, who died in a Georgia prison when I was four. All I knew about him was the arthritic stiffness in her hip, which he fractured pushing her down a flight of stairs, and the misalignment of her once broken nose. I knew my father by the crow's feet at her temples, the sarcasm of her smile, and her hoarse laughter. My mother laughed a lot. When she did, her sparkly eyes bored through you in case you missed the blackness of her humor. But where it came from or how she earned it, you kind of knew not to ask.

To be a kid in Mendocino was something else again. We had to draw those edges twice and three times, till they blurred enough to open the spaces of an uncertain belonging. The world could be a frightening place when you lived around adults who felt like fugitives in it, and who'd given up wanting from it their fair share of success or recognition. It also didn't help knowing we'd have to make our way in that world one day, whether we liked it or not.

There wasn't much to keep us in Mendocino. Work was hard to come by: too little timber for the mills to stay open, collapsing salmon stocks and dwindling crab catches for the fishermen, not enough construction jobs for all the cement workers and drywall hangers out there. I knew people who grew medical marijuana (if they cared to be legitimate about it), harvested sea vegetables, or made themselves into professional urchin divers, but the writing was still on the wall. We felt caught in holding patterns, unable to stay but afraid of leaving. The frustration in that made us moody and unpredictable. We were prone to lash out and attracted to extremes. This willfulness was easy enough to excuse, and not only because we felt wronged by circumstances beyond our control. We sensed in it a strange fidelity to the nature that haunted us in Mendocino. That was why the things we did, or rather the things we fucked up and the hopes we failed, could feel so right sometimes, so moon-pulled like those restless tides. They attuned us to the place we loved even as the price of our fidelity was gradually becoming higher than anyone could pay.

On summer days a bunch of us would gather at the middle school court and play basketball. No one ever planned it out beforehand. For some reason we had more fun when it was accidental like that. You could count on Jordi being there, practicing his shot for hours on end. But if the weather was right, warm and not too windy, you only had to wait and enough people would eventually turn up for a game. If they didn't, you could still shoot around with whoever did come and let the day undo any ambition.

I remember those games as they were at their best. Everyone came together in the right way, and we eased each other into another dimension of focus and pleasure. Time slowed down almost to a standstill, opening out as wide as the sky we felt a little more enclosed by, and the day became a bona fide event.

It was a delicate spell to maintain. It could vanish if even one person failed to keep his pride and temper in check. To be honest it mostly vanished, even if the times it didn't stood out in our minds all the more for their rarity. Jordi grew frustrated if he missed a shot he shouldn't. Fox, who would play in his cowboy hat and pointy boots if he could, started pushing people around and picking fights. Zach gave up, lapsed into silence, even lost interest altogether and wandered off the court to smoke a joint. Cooper, the guy who never said a word about himself, turned into a freight train on the court, losing any sense of restraint.

There didn't seem to be a way around this unraveling. Even when we tried not to, we ended up trying too hard and the result was the same. This may have been my problem most of all, since I was the playmaker, the one who made other things happen. My skill was peripheral vision. I had to see everybody at once, sensing the possibilities in a look or a turn, a stop or a start, a missed step or a sudden spurt. I also had to take account of people's foibles, their conceits, their doubts, their grievances, their self-love. I might have known more about these things in them than even they did.

But I could over-think the game, too. If I wasn't careful, I could take myself right out of the moment with the best of them, straining for an excellence I knew betrayed me to my own pride, my own willfulness. Then I was the one who unraveled. I was the one who upset the balance of action and passion, motion and rest, to which I fancied myself so committed. Of course, the only thing to be done at that point was to pull back and start again. We had to remember that we learned from mistakes. They even made us better, if we let them. Maybe this was the secret of those games, the reason why they were both so transitory and so doomed. For them to be memorable, they first had to be acts of forgiveness.

One sign that the day was going well would be a visit by Ryder, who embodied the mercurial spirit of those games better than anyone. He was a willowy tall black man with matted dreadlocks, one of the many drifters in Mendocino who made their beds on Big River Beach and in the cemeteries, next to the dead ladies and sea captains from a hundred years ago. He appeared, when he did, from the baseball field or the vacant lot across the street, peeling off his checked coat and loping onto the court, ready to join in.

Ryder didn't speak much when he played. The game had a more private meaning for him, bound up with circles, curves, swoops, and spirals. He moved like a slowly hovering helicopter, all elbows and knees, his shoulder blades rotating, his hips and belly completely supple. In his mind there was some intrigue, some space of urgency or alarm that only he knew about, even if it still depended on the actions of those surrounding him. He was also a receptive player, as alert as I wanted to be to the little fleeting coincidences that any game was constantly throwing up to our attention. I had a lot to learn from Ryder in this respect.

We liked having him around, even though he was erratic at times, to the point of making us wonder about his sanity. But we looked past the discomfort this caused, because we also needed him. We had the makings of a good varsity team our senior year, and, for reasons I'll get to later, there was a lot of pressure on all of us to keep on top of our games. We needed as much practice as we could get with better play-ers, and that wasn't easy in a small town. Sometimes we'd play with older people, graduates from the high school still trying to figure out what to do with their lives. They were quicker and hungrier than we were, but they didn't have a lot to teach us. In fact, playing with guys like that was often counter-productive, since they almost couldn't help commu-nicating their own inability to move on, or out, of the places and habits they knew best. We needed the same thing they did: courage to face the world, to go beyond a shared fear of the unknown. Ryder stepped right out from that world, however broken it might have left him once, in some place too dark really for coming back.

My mother and I lived in a small Queen Anne's cottage next to Point Cabrillo, a couple miles north of town. She operated a kennel in the yard. The proceeds from that kept us fed and moving, although we often had to struggle to stay ahead of our bills. The cottage was pretty run down. It seemed like I was always fixing leaks in the roof, repairing propane generators or water pumps, and replacing pipes so old they crumbled in my hand when I dug them out. This gave me a feel for things most people don't ever have to learn, like how much weight a board will take before it snaps or how much you can twist copper before it strips. I learned to be practical that way.

We were good at keeping each other company. In our loneliness, we had to be. Our favorite pastime was playing the mandolin together. My mother was pretty handy with it, and over years of listening to her renditions of "Foggy Mountain" and "Orange Blossom Special," I got the hang of it, too, in a haphazard fashion. I never learned how to read music, but I could hear a keynote and keep a tune in my head well enough to play along or improvise. We listened to the radio a lot at night, flat-picking the guitar licks in rock songs and mixing in bluegrass turnarounds, playing down by the bridge Earl Monroe-style.

The mandolin was the perfect instrument for a guy with my temperament. It had more than enough drive and bounce for solos, but it fit best in the background, streaming eighth notes through a tune, adding tone to other instruments or voices. It accompanied more than it led, although being so rhythmic, it also helped to balance the different parts of a song, seamlessly meshing the melody with the beat.

My mother learned how to play as a teenager in South Carolina, although not, as you might expect, in hill country attending hootenannies and barn dances. Her family was as upper class as you could be in Greenville. She grew up riding horses around polo grounds and holding her fork the right way at the dinner table. But you'd never guess it looking at her. Those grooved wrinkles in her leathery skin made you think of a field hand more than a debutante. She could care less about finery or convention.

How she changed like that you might never know, although it made some sense when you considered my prim and proper grandparents, who were so set in their ways they made rebellion inescapable. I met them one time growing up. They came for a visit and found our little cottage so dispiriting they checked into a hotel rather than stay with us. God and hygiene seemed to be the only topics they cared to discuss. In my child's mind, they seemed less like real people than characters in books. I think my mother had a hard time believing in them at all.

She did better around the likes of Ryder, who fit an upside down idea she held to that crazy people were sane and sane people were crazy. As confusing as this might be, there was a finely tuned moral reasoning behind it. My mother taught me to hew through prejudice to the human quality in people, no matter how far at sea they, or you, might be. She would say this quality resembled quicksilver: intense and elusive, it resisted every shape, every outline. It disliked having to exist. But it couldn't be denied any more than it could be forced. However exasperating, it had to be lived or worked with in people and in yourself, too. It was like that uncanny feeling you had in Mendocino of never quite standing on solid ground.

2

Rumor spread fast the day Chase MacMillan first arrived at school. Everybody was talking about him. He was 6'3" tall, lean, and almost scarily self-assured. We found out later that he came to town from Los Angeles, which made sense. You felt a kind of Hollywood glamour in him. He looked like someone you should know already. What he found interesting, you wanted to find interesting, too. You resented him because you admired him, and because he didn't feel your admiration meant he owed you something. Right away we could tell it would be hard to put him in a place that allowed us to keep our pride.

If we needed proof that Chase would change everything for us, he provided it in the gym at lunch, where we normally stole an hour to shoot around or play a game or two in our street clothes. Fox and Cooper were taking turns running at the basket for the most spectacular dunks they could muster when Chase entered through the front entrance to mingle with the 9th graders who were shooting at the other end.

The first time he rose up and lifted the ball into the air, I knew even before it sliced the net that he was good, very good, at the game. The rule in those casual shooting situations was you kept the ball as long as you didn't miss, and he kept that ball, hitting over and over again from all around the perimeter. Fox and Cooper started running even harder at the basket, but their aggression just sharpened the contrast between their movements and Chase's relaxed and methodical style. At last I broke through the tension between us and walked down the court to ask him if he wanted to play a game of two-on-two. He thought about it a second, eyes skittering from me to Fox to Cooper, before he finally agreed.

After terse introductions, I paired with him and we began the ritual of the game. As soon as Chase got the ball, he went hard to the basket and pulled up on Fox's off-balance shoulder for a jump shot. He set the tone of his own authority with that, and it would never vary. He had all the moves, inside and out. No one could touch him. I could see this flustering Fox, who before long had fallen back to his one advantage, brute strength. He forced Chase into driving attacks on the basket, where Cooper would collapse on him with the solidity of a heavy blade falling. But either Chase would flick the ball out to me or he'd manage by some improbable contortion of his body to slip through the defense anyway. I could see from my vantage point at the top of the key that he had a lot of spring in his legs and played much higher around the rim than any of us.

The game ended with Fox losing his temper altogether and shoving Chase to the floor. He crashed into the wall beneath the stage that opened at that end of the gym. Fox glared down at him, wanting some kind of confrontation, but struggling inside with that tacit code of male honor we all knew he'd violated. Chase slowly lifted himself to his feet, his every move calculated to defuse the tension. "I guess the game's over," he said with a nod at me, walking off down the floor to the entrance. All we could do was stare at his departing back.

I'd never seen anything quite like the skill Chase showed that first day. It impressed me, and it also scared me a little. I couldn't say why exactly. I think it stirred up a feeling of envy as well as respect. It made me feel my own limitations, just the way it must have done for Fox and Cooper. I didn't like what that said about me any more than I knew how to ignore or stop it. I did know it pointed to something in my own character that I would need to figure out better than I had.

I saw Chase leave after school, and impulsively I followed him down the hill on which the high school stood. A part of me wanted to tell him not to worry about Fox, but another part held back. I wasn't sure I wanted him to see that envy or whatever it was I felt without understanding. I didn't know if I could hide it either.

I let up halfway down the stairs and watched him get into a blue BMW 2002, one of those hat-shaped cars I always liked, which was parked next to the arts center across the street. The fog had socked the whole town in that day, rolling furiously in place through the trees and over the wood frame houses and water towers. From its shelter, I watched him start the engine, swing around in the opposite direction, and drive off. I remained for a moment afterward, still uncertain in my mind. I saw a fire burning in the arts center's pottery kiln. A man was moving around in the yard there, putting pots and cups onto shelves. In the distance, a foghorn measured out the swell in mournful blasts.

Later that same afternoon I took a bunch of dogs on a walk, something I did almost every day to help my mother with the kennel. I opened the cages and led them through a neighboring trailer park, composed of a semicircular dirt road lined with mobile homes and cottages, to a flat field of mown green grass with a few campsites and fire pits in it.

I stopped to say hello to Miriam, a deaf woman who lived in the trailer closest to the field. I'd begun learning the basics of sign language from her, so she didn't have to write me notes as much when we talked. I didn't stay long, though, since her husband Daniel, a fisherman, was there, and he seemed more ill-at-ease than he usually did. I had the feeling he didn't like me all that much. He might not have liked anybody, however. He mostly preferred to be alone.

From the field, a path cut into massive headlands that stretched almost a mile to the lighthouse on Point Cabrillo. The place was a preserve by then, as wide open as when it belonged to the lighthouse keepers, who had, in addition to making sure the lamp burned in the tower and the compressors were powered in the signal room, operated a viable farm. I think they mostly raised livestock. Of course, that was a long time ago. The lighthouse had been automated decades before.

I spent a lot of time in that preserve, me and a pack of dogs. I liked to pick out networks of deer paths and lose myself not only in its farthest reaches but in its seasons and cycles. It gave me a feeling for how interconnected things were: for the wind sweeping seeds from the grasses or shaking clouds of pine dust loose from the cones; for the vectors of cross-pollination linking up burrs, bats, peas, vetch, cow parsnip, moths, and the gut of a gray fox. It all absorbed me the way a kid might put together a picture puzzle, only the picture was the world. It surrounded me and implied me at the same time.

That day I ended up by a catch pond. I sat for a while on the lip of the weir with my arms wrapped around my knees, right at the edge of the still water rimmed all around by blackberry bushes. When I was a boy, it spooked me to look down in that pond's frozen underworld of submerged deadwood and yellowed algae. It had a nightmarish quality. I imagined there were drowned bodies in its muddy bottom. It gave my thoughts, still back on that hillside watching Chase drive off, a darker turn. They went something like this: because that pond was the locus of a whole system of flows, the gravitational center of the headland as a watershed, a living and breathing habitat, it followed that everything tended to find there its zero degree. Me, too, since I was just as much a part of that habitat as anything else. Gravity acted both on me, as a physical force, and in me, as desires and needs.

But then I wondered if I really understood what I was doing when I came to that pond as if to myself. Was I in fact seeing my own nature all that clearly? I considered myself a good observer, but I had also begun to feel, in myself observing, a reluctance to look too squarely at those desires and needs. I worried that my walks into the preserve were more like excuses than discoveries now. I used ospreys, blue herons, and meadowlarks as pretexts for hiding from myself. Which meant, given everything else I believed to be true about nature, that I wasn't seeing much at all.

These reflections soon had me tied up in knots, so before long I put them aside and moved on to the lighthouse, with its stately Fresnel lens throwing colors of the rainbow out the lantern room as it turned. It was driven by an electric motor now, but the original clockwork mechanism had been preserved inside: a weight descending through each floor of the tower on a heavy chain, which the lighthouse keeper cranked onto a turning drum every two hours or so. Even then the rate of rotation never wavered; the flash of light over the ocean at night was a signature of the place, recognized on nautical charts a good fifteen miles out by ships crisscrossing the coast or bending slowly into the open sea and the ports of Asia. Of course, electronic satellite systems had rendered the lighthouse more or less obsolete as a navigation aid. Only a few local fishermen still counted on it, and then only out of habit or nostalgia. Nobody really looked out the window anymore when they wanted to find out where they were.

I walked back up the road this time, past the signal building, the pump house, the water tanks, and the three residences that had been restored along with the lighthouse itself, all painted in beige with red trim. The compound had been turned into a research center operated by the Coast Guard, or the government anyway. I assumed as much from the different people staying there over the years. They seemed like scientists, since I'd often seen them scuba diving around the reefs or observing sea lions and dolphins from motorboats.

To my surprise, that day I saw Chase's blue car parked behind one of the houses. I slowed down, struck by the coincidence and curious to find out more. A moment later, a man appeared in the yard, gathering firewood from a small shed. He was as tall as Chase, with a shock of white hair, and he seemed preoccupied, like someone accustomed to giving long and serious thought to what he did. I imagined he wouldn't take very well to being interrupted, but I shot past my scruples and called out to him anyway. I asked if he had a son who went to the high school. He nodded and headed back inside with the load of wood. Chase came out the front door onto the porch. I thought by his hesitation that he couldn't place me.

"We played that game today," I reminded him.

"I know."

A crease of a smile told me he considered my assumption of his forgetfulness a little odd. We stood in awkward silence. He noticed the dogs. "What are you doing?"

I told him about the kennel. He took in the news with a wondering look. "You live nearby then," he inferred, as if he had a hard time believing anybody could.

"By the trailer park," I said, pointing back up the headlands. "You pass right by it before you turn into the preserve." I nodded at the house behind him. "You, too?"

He glanced back through the door he'd left open. "My father's here on a grant. He's an underwater physicist. He studies bioacoustics."

"Huh," I said. "What's that exactly?"

"It's hard to describe. He spends a lot of time on whales."

This I understood. Gray whales migrated back and forth along the coast every year, and Point Cabrillo was a particularly good place to observe them.

"How long are you staying?" I asked.

"Till the end of the school year."

I paused a moment too long for comfort. I was finding all this a lot to take in.

"You've got a nice shot," I said, changing the subject. "You must have played before, where you come from."

"The Pacific Palisades."

"I bet they hated to see you go."

He rubbed the back of his head. "I might have been more trouble than I was worth."

"Trouble?"

I saw him regret the need for an explanation. "I haven't been too focused lately."

"You must be thinking about playing in college."

"Yeah, well. . ." This seemed to mire him in difficulties. His answer was a little too cryptic. "Then I'd have to focus."

"You're not liable to get much exposure here," I said, ignoring his evasive tone. "Not like you're used to, I mean."

He guessed what I had in mind. "I wasn't thinking I'd play anymore."

"Why not? We could use a guy like you."

"I don't know." His father called out to him. He glanced back inside again, welcoming the distraction. "It's time for dinner."

"I'm going to keep on you about it," I said affably. "And if I don't, our coach will. He can be very persuasive. He used to play himself, once. You'd like him."

I started calling the dogs. They had drifted off over the fields.

"Take it easy," he said.

"You, too."

He went inside and I bounded up the road, feeling a lot better than I had before. The walk home was almost buoyant. New things didn't happen that often in Mendocino.

Chase and his father came to town, in part, because Chase's mother had died. He told me later, once we became better friends, that she'd locked herself in a bathroom and overdosed on pills she took for chronic stomach pain. He blamed her poor health on the stress of her career as a fashion model. I gathered from this that she was beautiful and successful, the kind of woman everybody desired, and the way she died especially tragic. It had hit Chase so hard he quit school, turned moody and reckless, and burned himself out in parties and drugs. This was another reason they'd come to Mendocino: to change the scene of his willful self-destruction.

I started inviting him to the middle school when I thought we might get a game going. It didn't happen so often with the end of summer vacation. Fox played football, so he rarely showed up once his season started, and everyone else, except for Jordi, was distracted with school. But we still managed to play on some weekends. The games grew pretty intense the first times Chase showed up, mostly because it hurt to admit he was the best player on the court. His superiority meant we had to overcome our vanity, and no one does that without a struggle. I kept telling everybody he made us better. That was true enough, if we let ourselves rise to his level instead of dragging him down to ours. But it would take a while for this to sink in.

Coach appeared in his Buick town car one afternoon to cement Chase's place with us. He drove it right into the playground and parked beside the court, smoking one of his customary Erik cigarettes, or cigarillos I guess they were called. From the driver's seat he watched us play, noting all the little details of the game with the cool concentration of an expert. Basketball, for him, was a way of life. He'd been living it and breathing it since before we were born.

He'd heard about Chase from Jordi, of course, so we knew he'd come to see for himself what good fortune had graced the Mendocino Cardinal varsity team. When Chase knifed through the key with one particularly athletic stretch toward the basket, showing the kind of horizontality I recognized as what Coach was always trying to get from us, he threw his head back in a growl of laughter. We knew he was impressed.

That basket also ended the game, so we all dispersed. Some moved toward the water faucet, others to the ice plant on the bank that lined one side of the court. Only Chase and I continued to shoot around. At one point, Coach called him over to the car.

"Where'd you learn to play like that?" I heard him say, his arm resting steadily against the door. Above the wrist there was the blurred tattoo of a screaming eagle.

"LA."

"You have to get more under your shot, though. The ball sits too much on the palm. That's why there's not enough spin when you let go. It glides more than it spins, like a flying saucer. When you don't drill it, it bangs wide off the rim."

He extinguished the Erik in his car ashtray and got out. "I'll show you."

The first thing you noticed about Coach was his physical presence, the poise across his shoulders, the looseness in his big hands. Although in his late fifties, he moved like a much younger man, with a decision as controlled as it was supple and arousing. His expression was shrewd, calculating. He sized people up more than he looked at them.

I passed him the ball, which he didn't so much take as vacuum in. "Watch me." He bent his knees, bobbing lightly, and crouched a little. His body was all self-contained, like a man in a cockpit. He slowly lifted his shoulders, the ball curling up and off his fingers. Only he didn't shoot it at the basket. He let it revolve in the air a few feet and bounce back into his hands.

"You see how it does that?" he said. "No matter where or when you let it go, at that moment it's gotta spin like that." He handed Chase the ball. "Shoot a jump shot, and look at the ball when you do."

Jordi came up beside me on the court. Glancing sideways at him, I could see he was jealous of his Dad's interest in Chase. We both watched the ball arc through the air. There was something glassy about it, frozen, even if Chase's aim was spot on.

"It's flat," he conceded.

"You're not under it enough," Coach said again. "You're not drawing the force through your legs up from the ground, or through the ground."

Other people had come back to the court and stood nearby, listening in. Coach's voice rose a decibel or two.

"You all think of shooting a basketball in terms of half a circle," he said, "but actually it's a whole circle. The other half is under the ground. It comes up out of your feet, runs through your fingers and the basket, and goes back into the ground. It's a cycle, or a circuit."

He took the ball and shot it a few times, exaggerating his own fluidity.

"You look at any athlete you admire," he said, "and you'll see he's working inside that circle. Doesn't matter what kind of athlete he is. He's working there *all* the time, whatever he's doing." He handed Chase the ball and stepped away, suddenly annoyed at hearing himself speak. I think he sensed a weakness in it that he didn't like. The lesson, anyway, was over. "Why don't you guys play."

He went to the Buick and lit another Erik from his pack. Then he leaned against the door and watched us choose teams.

⚡

Everybody called him Coach, but his name was Ray Ellis. He'd cast his spell on all of us from the time we were middle school students. That was when he first started coaching the varsity team. He'd been in Mendocino for a while before that, though, hiding from his own secrets. I found out one of them when, not quite a year before the day he met Chase, I came over to his house on the outskirts of town to watch a basketball game on television. At one point, his wife, Anastasia, a tall big-boned woman who came from Vladivostok, Russia, sat down on the living room sofa and complained about her bad back. Coach ordered Jordi to get her a shot of Wild Turkey.

"Bring me a Sprite, too, while you're at it," he added, looking at me with sparkly eyes. Both of us remembered practice the previous day, when he was particularly hard on me. "Sure would like some of that Wild Turkey for my back," he said, in a conciliatory tone. "You know why I can't?" He glanced at Anastasia, seeking permission, it seemed to me, for the disclosure he was about to make. "I'm an alcoholic, Woody," he said, shifting uneasily in his seat. "I don't mind admitting it. I made a mistake once. I got in over my head. Now I have to watch myself. . .like a hawk. I can't be as free as I'd like. I have to be tough on myself. It's why I'm tough on you, too." He nodded at the television. "It's also why this game's not just a game. Sometimes it's a matter of life and death."

Such confessions made you like Coach, or sense in him circumstances sufficiently hard to warrant your sympathy, even when he got mad at you on the court. His disciplined approach to the game might hit like a hurricane, but its relation to those circumstances made you want to understand, even when you just couldn't. I felt them most in the tough way he treated Jordi. We might screw up completely and still hear it said, "Rome wasn't built in a day," but Jordi never had any leeway. The standards were much higher. Jordi also lacked the athletic ability of his father, or even some of us. He had to work harder to get the same results, and Coach kept pushing him right up to his limits.

Jordi handled the pressure without complaint, accepting it in the terms Coach himself sometimes used, as a backhanded kind of care, a preparation for the hostility that he believed would inevitably be visited upon him in this world. If anything, Jordi tended to relay the same discipline, or the same torment, to those around him. He made it worse, in fact, because he was also Christian and mixed his insistence on us to practice with an evangelical zeal he learned, I think, more from his mother, who belonged to the local Baptist church. This could make it hard to feel sorry for him, even if his heart was in the right place.

Coach had that earnest religious side as well, but you could see it was secondary for him. His faith was laid over other personal concerns. Much more than virtue or salvation, it was respect Coach wanted. You could feel he'd been starved of it for a long time. I gathered from what Jordi told me that he grew up in farm towns on the Texas-Oklahoma border, poor and resentful but very talented at basketball. He won a scholarship to the University of Oklahoma, where he was starting guard and an All-American his final season. He had a decent shot at the NBA after that, but then he received a draft notice from the army. Despite his reputation and promise, they refused to give him an easy out or even a deferment. Instead of signing a million-dollar contract, he went to Vietnam and fought in the war.

On his return, he hoped to pick up his career where he left off, trying out for various teams. But the window of opportunity had closed on him, and he never got the break he needed. For years he bounced around semi-professional leagues until he had to admit he was washed up as a player. That's when he started coaching. He hoped it, too, would become a career for him, but he never made it very far there either. It must have been then that the drinking turned into a problem. Jordi was vague about the timing of that. But we all knew from the long slide to high school coach in Mendocino that nothing had worked out for Coach quite the way he wanted. He once told me his life was two steps forward, three steps back. He was always walking into the wind.

3

As it came closer to basketball season, I started preparing everyone for the sacrifices ahead. Jordi and I competed for the role of team captain, both officially and off the court, but his ideas of discipline left most of us cold. I was the better coordinator, mostly because I liked finding common grounds. I liked sensing where people were in their minds and hearts. I was a pretty good psychologist. I knew how to draw my friends out of their insecurities by turning their reasons to give up or float back on them. I wove a vision of basketball as art out of Zach's native languor. I played Fox's pride against his pessimism. I made them both feel the energy in their own evasions. Even at our most confident, we could cave in, grow weirdly passive, and submit to higher forces like a wolf gives its throat to a superior foe.

But as much as this timidity might hold us back, I didn't think it was just a weakness. The man coming to be in all of us was still a kid at heart. He stood in his power on the slippery rocks of a minus tide, looking for the hermit crabs and abalone shells of a playful spontaneity. It was when we couldn't find that spontaneity anymore, when the connection between kid and man was cut, that we turned against ourselves, gave up, or flared out. When we did find it, on the other hand, power became graceful, the will subtle and clear. The important thing was not to cut that connection. To my mind, growing up was less a matter of stages we went through than the right way to keep the past alive.

Admittedly, I didn't always do this right way the justice it deserved. There were also wrong ways to keep the past alive. I saw this more in my relations to girls than in my behavior on the court. I tended to hide my feelings when they were sexual. Instead of risking rejection by letting others know what they were, I'd nurse secret crushes.

At that time it was Suzanne Miles I liked this way. She was a fellow senior who aspired to be a musician and had such a good voice she sometimes sang at the bar in town where my mother parked herself on Saturday nights. I started seeing her in a romantic light on the occasions when I'd drop by to pick my mother up.

I saw Suzanne every day in the 5th period calculus class we took, eagerly awaiting the few minutes before the bell rang when I could ask about her day. She had a protean personality, constantly moving on to some new interest that she never tired of explaining. Her moods shifted and changed with her eclectic tastes. I loved how she dressed: in vintage clothes, with long colorful scarves and funky hats.

She might have been too flamboyant, trying too hard to match an idea of herself as a performer, but she was never conceited about it. She knew how to dispel insincerity with a look or a gesture. When she touched my wrist to say good-bye, or even occasionally drew her cheek close to mine and kissed the air by my neck, the quiver of flesh or grazed hair would stay with me all through the day. . .and night, too.

For the life of me, though, I couldn't tell her how I felt. Even when I made up my mind to try, I ended up losing my nerve at the last minute. On the surface this shyness didn't fit my character at all. I was able to hide my feelings so well because no one thought of me as shy. I threw up the screen of affable Woody, easy in himself and tolerant of others, but behind it I felt perfectly split, like two people in one, and neither side entirely honest with the other.

The closest I came to asking Suzanne out on a date was when she asked me. She'd just given me an oiled buffalo hide hat for my birthday, which I would wear almost everyday for the rest of that year. When I said it was "perfect for a mandolin player," she had the idea of us playing together. "I have a couple songs that need a mandolin arrangement," she said.

My heart jumped, and I started in right away with my usual evasive tactics. "Talk to my mother," I told her. "She's the one who's really good."

"I'm sure you're better than you think you are." She fixed me with a knowing look. "At a lot of things, too."

That left me no other choice but to shrug my shoulders and say, "Let's do it."

But that was as far as I could get. I didn't bring it up again and hoped she wouldn't ask, although I started practicing the mandolin more seriously than I ever had before. The result was I became too aware of my shortcomings and lost much of my usual touch. My mother noticed right away. When I confessed my problem to her, she said the only thing to do was to stay relaxed and be yourself.

"And if you can't, then wait until you can," she advised with that faint Southern lilt in her voice, *cay-unn* sounding almost like two syllables instead of one. "You know what Harry Houdini once said: 'Love laughs at locksmiths.'"

"What does that mean?!"

"I don't know," she said, as if she didn't. Dispensing advice wasn't her strong suit. "You can't lock the heart in anymore than you can pick its lock, I guess."

I didn't see how that was going to help me out of my troubles, but at least I had another reason to delay, and I saw from how I dug in to my own reluctant nature that I might very well never get together with Suzanne and play music. Once again I'd bury my desire in the catch pond of my boyish heart and go back to the role of good old genial Woody. As it happened, though, I wouldn't have to find out just how true this was.

ξ

A short while later there was a school dance. The gym had been turned over to revolving disco balls, and a local band played covers of pop songs from the stage. As usual on these occasions, everybody got very drunk and very high, turning the night into shivaree. I wandered around as my usual free agent, talking to people who wouldn't otherwise talk to each other and enjoying this ability I had to connect different types.

Mine was a formal feeling. I looked to the structure in things, in relationships, even in places. I loved that old gym for this reason. It had served the town well as a gathering place, even if everybody hated it. The booster club was trying to get the school to tear it down and build a new one. Coach was particularly fierce in pushing for this. He gave speeches at school board meetings and leaned on the principal for action. But I preferred it just the way it was, a relic from another era, with dark brown floorboards, blood red paint in the keys, and rafters that creaked in the offshore winds that swept up from the headlands around the town. On the wall by the scoreboard were banners from all the years Mendocino teams had won league titles, going back to 1919. That gym did more than foster a sense of community: it rooted us in time and history. It made the feeling that we belonged to a particular place more durable.

But any pleasure I took of this rooted kind ended that night when I saw Suzanne and Chase dancing to Pearl Jam's "Better Man" on the floor. Their obvious intimacy cut all the way through me, and the shock of it made every idea I had about myself, about what I liked and why, vanish into thin air. It wasn't just a collapse of confidence. It was more like a loss of consciousness. For a moment I even wondered if I'd be able to stay on my feet. Isolated all of a sudden in a self I could no longer grasp, I felt emptied out, reduced to nothing. I was just this pure witness of other people's desires, or rather of my own desire taken up and acted on by others like it was some kind of spectacle. That was the worst part. Their desire took mine from me. The more they enjoyed themselves, the more displaced I felt. The more attractive they seemed, the more devoured I felt in an absolute loneliness.

My only thought was to take the bottle of Bacardi 151 from Fox and get drunk. Fox, as shrewd as his name might suggest when he wanted to be, quickly guessed the cause of my distress and began running Chase down as a poacher of other guy's girls. He did it with relish, too, because it simultaneously pulled me into that despair where he sought the resource of home and needed the company of others. But whatever I needed right then, it wasn't this kind of fellowship. I took no comfort in the revenge Fox thought up for me either: luring Chase to the dusty storage rooms in the basement and beating him to a pulp. I couldn't see how that was going to help me feel less alone or return to me anything like the desire Chase and Suzanne showed on the dance floor. Just the opposite. It would kill that desire for everyone.

I tried to tell Fox as much, in too confused a fashion to have much effect. Zach would have better luck, it turned out, and not by anything he said, just by reeling through the crowd all by himself, like Johnny Depp on a pirate ship. I think he even wore a three-pointed hat, along with his dad's green velvet dinner jacket, which was about two sizes too big. His crazy masquerade brought us both back to our senses; at least Fox forgot his plan to beat up Chase. It reminded me that there was more health in insouciance than resentment. Nothing was so serious that you couldn't laugh about it, at least when enough time had passed.

I took this to heart as best I could, but it didn't make things any easier in that gym as I tried to avoid Chase and Suzanne. I tracked their movements despite myself. I knew where they were at almost every moment.

In the end, I couldn't stand it and escaped to the open air, slipping out the front door to sit in the cold and the dark on the bleachers that faced the football field. There I found Jordi and Cooper talking quietly over the relentless pounding of the music inside. It shook the whole frame of the gym.

I slid onto the bench beside them and looked out toward the tall windswept brakes of cypress trees that rimmed the field on two sides. I wasn't sure I liked sharing that night with Jordi and Cooper. They were both too bottled up for their own good. They took things in more mysteriously than either Fox or Zach. They rarely surprised you, but you never knew for sure just what they were thinking. Cooper, in particular, had a spooky withdrawn air about him. He kept to himself as a rule. I don't think any of us had ever even been to his house, wherever that was at the moment. He and his dad moved around a lot.

This fact struck me, at that moment, as an injustice. "Coop, why don't I know anything about you?" I said, sounding more confrontational than I wanted. "I mean, who are you, really?" I waved a hand in front of his face. "Where are you?"

He could tell I'd had too much to drink, and he knew we were friends, or at least I hoped he did. In the back of my mind I promised myself that I would apologize to him the first sober chance I got.

He peered hard into the night. "You don't want to know," he replied. "I'm a ghost."

Jordi and I looked archly at each other. He said it like he meant it.

The next night the five of us, Fox, Zach, Jordi, Coop, and I, piled into Fox's truck and drove to the bowling alley in Fort Bragg. The town was about eight miles up the coast, set away in simple platted streets from the ocean behind an abandoned lumber mill. I didn't much feel like going, but I also needed to close ranks a little after that dance. I needed to remind myself of the things that mattered to me and the allegiances I still had to the place where I lived. As undermined in them as I might have felt, it seemed reasonable enough to assume that I wasn't seeing things any more clearly after I saw Chase and Suzanne dancing than before. I hoped, at any rate, that the truth lay somewhere in between.

At the alley we saw a few of the guys who played for the high school in Fort Bragg, rolling their lines on the far end. They were more redneck than rednecks, with names like Brett Kettleman and Wade Sumner. We thought of ourselves as a little superior despite the fact they'd always thrashed us on the basketball court. They tensed up when they noticed us, feeling proprietary in their own town but not otherwise disposed to make an issue out of it. They were more interested in showing off in front of the girls who sat behind the lanes in molded plastic chairs.

One, in particular, we all knew as the sexiest girl on the coast. Her name was Sky. She was celestial in her appeal all right, with sumptuous blond hair and arresting blue eyes. As a cheerleader she was their secret weapon, since she tended to keep the whole male persuasion in the gym distracted with her enlivening kicks.

We liked to say that we might not beat Fort Bragg on the court, but we were hands down the better looking of the two teams. Fox was the guy girls noticed, brawny and brash. He fit best into the super-masculine culture of loggers and fishermen on the coast. We noticed Sky casting sly glances his way while we set up to play. Zach, completely fearless, started waving her over. "Come on!" he said. "Ditch those Neanderthals." He knew they couldn't hear.

"Don't get them started," I warned.

"What kind of a name is Sky, anyway?" he wondered. "No name at all, that's what. Nobody's *named* Sky. It's like calling somebody Thing. Or Circle. Or Handle. Or Branch."

"I'd fly in her sky," Fox crooned, to general hilarity.

We started playing, and the early rounds went without a hitch, them on their side, us on ours. But then I noticed Zach had wandered off to the snack bar and stood impishly at the counter next to Sky. I could tell by his repeated glances at us while they talked that he was spinning some kind of yarn about our intentions there. When his insinuations bordered on rude, as they often did, she broke away with bemused smiles, wisely I thought, and returned to the other end of the alley with a few bottles of soda in her hands. Zach sauntered back to our lane.

"What'd you say?" Fox demanded.

"I said you thought she was hot."

"No way!"

"I said you wanted to get in her pants."

"Fuck you!"

"Dude, she asked me for your number."

Fox stared. "You're shitting me."

Zach shook his head, laughing. "I'm shitting you," he admitted. "But I did ask if she wanted to meet up with us later, at the Caspar Inn."

"Are you crazy?" Fox was still taking Zach too seriously. "They'll never let us in." You had to be over twenty-one to get past the door at the bar there.

"I just wanted to see if she'd go for it."

Unfortunately, she told the Fort Bragg guys about his invitation, and they drew the worst possible conclusions about our motives. They started yelling across the lanes to get our own girls in our own town. Some of them were pissed off enough to move threateningly in our direction. At that point Fox stiffened and Zach started strutting around in little circles. Coop and Jordi rose to their feet, ready all at once and without a second thought for reaction. It's funny how we jettison fear and common sense when the stakes become our manhood. The mind cuts out, adrenalin takes over, and suddenly we're capable of anything.

There would have been some sort of confrontation if it hadn't been for Sky, who came up with the idea of settling the score with a game. She liked playing the manager, I could tell, maybe enough to like setting the scene a little beforehand as well. I didn't much trust this in her even if I did understand the impulse, but it was decided. Either we'd brawl or we'd bowl.

We moved into the lane next to theirs. As the two teams started warming up, I hung back behind the chairs and watched for signs of bad temper. Brett Kettleman looked like he might go berserk at any moment, but then he always did. After a while I noticed Sky quietly sidle up next to me. For some reason she felt like talking.

"Pretty silly, huh?" she said.

"What?"

"The games we play."

"Oh." I nodded.

"Boys will be boys."

There was a note of apology in her voice as she said this, drawn out into faint overtones of flirtation. Not that she meant it. She had the tastes of a conventional girl for the very "boys" she was criticizing. But maybe I interested her because I wasn't reacting the way she expected or was used to.

"You're not playing?" she asked.

"I'd rather watch."

"You're a 'lover, not a fighter'?"

The question was just playful enough, and the circumstances just unlikely enough, to prompt an honest response.

"I don't feel much like either one, lately."

"Why not?"

I suppressed an impulse to tell her about Chase and Suzanne. It would have been a relief right then to work out my troubles with a girl. Maybe she'd have some advice to give. But I opted for circumspection. "Seems like they go together. I can't be both at once."

"Desire is a little mean," she agreed, shrewdly grasping the core problem. "I figured that out a long time ago."

"You did?"

"The hard way."

"How so?"

She answered by telling me her stepfather tried to kill her. I cocked my head in surprise. "It's true!" she cried. "I swear to God. When I was twelve. I can't prove it, and only the two of us will ever know, because nobody believed me at the time. He just said he was drunk."

She waited to see how interested I was in hearing more. "Go on," I urged.

"One day, standing outside our garage," she said, "I saw him coming home from work in his truck. I was trying to fit the chain back on my bike, and I looked up just after he'd turned into the driveway, fast as he normally did. And right at the point I caught his eye through the windshield, I saw him pretend not to see I was there. I *saw* him decide to run me over."

"He ran you over?!"

"He broke my hip in two places. I was laid up in a cast for months afterward."

"Come on!" I said incredulously. "Why would he do a thing like that?!"

"It wasn't because he hated me," she said. "Just the opposite." At that point she brought out the reason for telling the story. "He did it because he *wanted* me. I wasn't exactly a girl anymore, but somebody he thought about in that way. You know? I could feel it whenever he looked at me. He hated the idea that he couldn't *have* me."

This sent my thoughts in a direction I hadn't anticipated. Desire wasn't mean because mean people confused love with aggression. It became mean in people who felt frustrated and denied. Deftly enough, Sky had shifted the burden of this desire onto guys who felt the way I did, guys who stood apart in envious witness of others. She didn't do it on purpose, of course. She wasn't suggesting I compare myself to her stepfather. But I guess because I also sensed her letting me know, with the confidence, that I was just a friend, not someone whose attention she would want or invite, I felt the association anyway.

I had no time to think about all this, however, because a shouting match had erupted between the two teams. Mendocino was already losing badly and Fox had taken to banging things around to assuage his wounded pride. Any hope of compromise ended when he shoved Brett Kettleman, who came back at him like a charging rhinoceros. The game turned into a fight that broke up only when the management threw us all out. I never got another chance to talk to Sky.

4

I'd have more time to think about my hurt feelings, though. Chase and Suzanne came out as a couple after that dance, and I had to get used to looking on while they grew more and more intimate with each other. Worse, since I was the one they both knew, I had to pretend I was happy for them. Once again I found myself caught in the diminished role of friend, observing desires in others that took me right out of my own.

It was beginning to feel a little unfair. Sure, I might've been too self-sacrificial for my own good. I might've been setting myself up in these situations, turning some secret shame or character flaw into a destiny. But people asked it of me, too. They needed a witness for their dramas, and good old Woody fit the bill more or less perfectly. If I didn't want to keep my distance, and my pride, by withdrawing into self-pity, it seemed the only thing I could do was submit to the inevitable.

So I submitted, not comfortably, but with as much grace as possible. I spent a lot of time with Suzanne and Chase, getting to know him better in particular. It wasn't easy on either of us. I could tell Chase didn't really fit in the world Suzanne and I shared. He grew impatient, even bored, when things happened in slow time. Then I felt a kind of pretense in him. I wouldn't exactly call it fake. He was a good actor. He brought out something true. But he didn't seem very connected either. I might have held this against him, or wondered because of it just how honest he was, had I been able to sort judgment from envy. Since I couldn't, though, it seemed only fair to give Chase the benefit of the doubt.

He did try to fit in. I gave him that. I could see him letting Mendocino change his habits, maybe even forge the connection I thought I'd missed in him. He had a good guide in Suzanne. She'd grown up there her whole life and knew things: what poison oak looked like, where to find the best mushrooms (not only the hallucinating kind), the dunes where wild strawberries grew, things like that. She also knew what it was to wake up cold and go a little hungry. As much as it hurt me to say, Chase had only to follow her lead and nature in Mendocino would open itself up to him in all sorts of ways.

A month into this new situation, the three of us went swimming with a few of Suzanne's friends at Deadman's, a bend in Big River a few miles inland where kids liked to go on hot days. It was only about two weeks before basketball practice officially started and Chase still hadn't said he would play. I tagged along mostly to keep him thinking about it. That was another reason I hung out with them so much. Coach had all but ordered me to keep the pressure on. He wanted Chase to play even more than I did.

I could see why Chase might hesitate, given what he was going through with his mother's death. Suzanne had also come out against it. She didn't like jocks or rednecks. She was a hippie at heart and preferred hanging out with people who started drum circles on the beach, wore hemp clothes, and listened to reggae. Inwardly I criticized her for that, even though I understood where she was coming from. But she didn't quite grasp what sports made possible. Basketball was an occasion for different people to mix up their beliefs, their values, also their injuries and prejudices. The background antagonisms of the place where we lived could get missed if you weren't looking for them. It was a little too easy in Mendocino to pretend there was only the present.

At one point, Chase and I swam off by ourselves to the other side of the river and climbed up to a rock ledge right over the water, watching Suzanne and her friends on the opposite bank passing a joint back and forth. I could see from our vantage point that Suzanne was shy about her body. She was big in the hips, with just a little too much weight in her thighs, and pale skin. I think this was one reason why she often wore long skirts. But she had lush brown hair and a beautiful face, very sculpted and classy in an old-fashioned way, like a girl in Pre-Raphaelite paintings. When she looked at you with her dark, penetrating eyes, you almost melted into the ground. I did, at any rate.

Chase had the perfectly cut body of a lifeguard. He showed no trace of self-consciousness. He could feel dressed even when he was naked. I envied that, since, by contrast, I was solid, muscular, and had a lot of body hair. This made it hard for me to take off my shirt in public. My mother said I was built like a lumberjack. I guess I took pride in that, but I never presumed to be the one everybody noticed either.

I wondered if Suzanne's little imperfections bothered Chase. He saw across the river exactly what I did. But he surprised me by saying he thought he was in love with her. The usual tension in his eyes softened. My heart sank.

"She's pretty special," I said stupidly.

"I've never met anyone like her. She's completely different from the girls I knew in LA, living in the mirror. I got really sick of that."

I took this cue to shift the topic away from Suzanne. "I can't say I've had much experience with those sorts of girls."

"They're fucking bitches," Chase said flatly.

I felt a lot of energy behind that. His anger surprised me. "Maybe they're just afraid," I said. "They're protecting themselves. Guys can be unpredictable sometimes."

"Just wait till a girl screws you over," he assured me. "Or more than one. After a while, you figure out that you'd better get a big picture view of women or you're dead. You won't even know what hit you. They'll leave you feeling like a complete idiot."

"Are guys different?"

"I never said we weren't assholes, too."

He didn't like my presumption that he was claiming some moral high ground. I guess it didn't necessarily follow from what he said. I took from this deeper pessimism that conventional male bonding didn't interest Chase.

"You don't like people much, do you?"

There might have been a trace of condescension in the smile this provoked. "Where I come from," he told me, "everybody's looking to get what they can. You are what you have to offer, and sometimes all you have to offer is what you are: your body, sex. What I've learned is there's nothing outside this exchange. Everybody's on the make, girls and guys, whether they admit it or not."

I listened with a grave demeanor, confused to hear an opinion like this coming from someone as inside that world as he seemed to be. "Are *you* on the make?"

This caught Chase off guard. He threw his head back and laughed. "Good question. I guess I'd have to say I am. But I'm tired of it, too. Tired of the game. I've been wondering lately if there's a way I might opt out, give up what I have, and stop caring about what I get. What do you think—is that possible?"

He eyed me sideways. Through the irony he seemed to be really asking. "What do I know?" I said with a shrug. "In the world you're talking about I suspect, I'm just someone with not much to offer."

"Not true," he countered. "Everybody's got something to offer. You start with what you have and make the most of it. That's the game. Just don't show your hand too easily. It's like poker."

"You have to bluff."

"Exactly."

"I'm only good at that when I'm not trying," I admitted. "The minute I try, I stop fooling people."

"It has to come naturally."

"But it isn't natural."

"That just means you have to practice."

He saw me wondering if I had the will for that. "The trick," he said, "is never to take what happens personally. If you don't take it personally, you don't get hurt. If you don't get hurt, then it really is just a game. You can even have fun with it. That's what my mother used to say about modeling."

He broke off, suddenly adrift in his memory of her. "But it is personal, isn't it?" I observed.

He glanced sharply at me. "It's brutal."

"Like what happened to your mom?"

I could feel him swimming in a wide arc around and out again. What he said next threw me off completely: "My mom was a fucking bitch."

The bitterness of these words, made worse because they were uttered in such a matter-of-fact way, revealed more of his state of mind than he wanted me, or anyone, to see just then. All at once he stood up and said, "I'm going back." He dove from the ledge into the green river water.

This conversation made me curious enough about Chase's mother to look her up online. My mother and I had gotten our first Internet connection a couple of years before, but neither of us used it much. She had a lot of prejudice to overcome about it. She didn't like the kind of interest it asked of you, sitting alone with a screen and absorbing random information. I had a better sense of what you could do with it. I knew kids who'd developed friendships through social media or found out about new music on different websites. It was a way of relating to the world that made you feel less parochial in a small town. By and large, though, I hadn't been able to find a rhythm with it either. I might use it to learn about birds or wildflowers, but mostly I just listened to the radio and practiced bluegrass turnarounds.

What I found out about Chase's mother, however, gave me my first inkling of why people could be so obsessive about the Internet. There must have been dozens of her images to look at. I saw her on covers of famous magazines and in advertisements for jeans, diamonds, chocolate, and champagne. I could hardly take my eyes off the suddenly mesmerizing screen. This went on for hours. It was so absorbing, and so abstract at the same time. I had this sense of getting very close to people, yet no one was there but me.

Friends of mine had said they were never more themselves than when online, but their eyes told me that they meant they could be what they wanted to be. Obviously, this wasn't the same thing as being yourself. Chase's mother was crazy beautiful, for instance, but she played all kinds of roles, too: vixen in lingerie, eager virgin in a wedding gown, corporate executive in a boardroom, socialite on a yacht, even revolutionary in a jungle. I couldn't tell sometimes if it was still the same woman from one image to the next. The only constants were her clear blue eyes, staring back at you in the pixelated light the same way every time. They had a transparency that might as easily signify emptiness as depth.

I found an obituary, too. There I learned summary facts: she grew up in Ann Arbor, Michigan, as the daughter of a prominent surgeon, moved to New York when she was seventeen, and became one of the most sought after models in the world, working with major fashion designers in America and Europe. After a decade spent leading a high-profile life, she married Chase's dad and settled down to raise a family. Recently, with the turn into middle age, she'd gotten involved in fundraising efforts on behalf of charity groups in Africa. Poor health, however, kept her more and more from the public eye. She passed away when she was forty-six.

Her name brought up links to the painkiller Oxycontin, an opiate derivative like heroin or morphine that had been developed for cancer patients. Doctors began prescribing it for all sorts of ailments, though, and over time people figured out how to dissolve the pill in a solution and inject it directly into the blood stream. Several prominent celebrities had developed an addiction to it. Chase's mother was mentioned.

Here I could see the dark side of that plastic capacity she had to embody different types of women: the event of her not bearing up under her own perfection, time filling in the body that was only ever implied behind the dazzling surface. And if she fell back to earth in the end, it was not as a victim of her own glamour. Chase's outburst at Deadman's suggested as much to me. The price of her success, of her presence on my screen, may rather have been the end of sympathy, or at least its hopeless tangle in the sort of steely criticism Chase made that day. I could see why my mother didn't care much for the Internet. Her instincts were canny enough. Whatever else it might give people in the way of connection, solace, or self-confidence, as a space of performance it had a kind of hatred built into it as well.

5

One afternoon Coach showed up at the middle school with a man I'd never seen before. He must have been 6'10" tall and all the ranginess in his body was still there, even though he'd lost his shape. You could guess why from the way he hobbled over with Coach to sit in the ice plant and watch us play. It looked like his knees might buckle out from under him at any moment.

Coach called Chase over when we finished our game. It turned out the man was a scout for the Stanford University basketball program and a former teammate of Coach's at Oklahoma.

Chase shook his hand, and they talked about the possibility of him coming to play for Stanford. I saw then what Coach was up to. All Chase had to do was put in a good season for us, and Stanford would keep an eye on him for a scholarship. The news had a rearranging effect on Chase's thoughts and priorities. It was enough for him to decide right then that he'd join the team. I'd told him Coach could be persuasive.

Everybody else on the playground was impressed, too, and more than a little jealous. None of us would have considered ourselves good enough to play at the college level. I don't think we'd even considered college. Fox might have had the size to play football, but he didn't have much in the way of grades or interest in school. He also had no better ideas. He talked all the time about what he wouldn't do after we graduated, but never about what he actually would do aside from more of the same work on his dad's ranch in the hills about fifteen miles from the coast. Fox had been repairing fences and baling hay there from the time he was six years old. It was the path of least resistance, and even that wasn't assured because the ranch was never profitable anyway, from what he'd told me. It kept Fox's family living on the land that his grandfather first purchased in the 1950s, but it could be a hardscrabble existence even in the best of times.

Nothing made Fox more wretched than the thought of staying on that ranch. He harbored a lot of shame about it. I'd seen just how much years before, when I'd gone up there with Zach to spend the night. At breakfast, we heard a field hand in the yard screaming about a cow having swallowed a piece of barbed wire. We all rushed outside to see what was going on and ran after his father through rain-flecked wind way out to the far side of a pasture, where the animal was trying to heave up the barbed wire in huge shudders.

The problem was a magnet they kept in one of the cow's stomachs. Fox said later they used it to prevent hardware disease. The magnet was attracting the barbed wire and pulling it back through the cow's gut. The field hand didn't know what to do, but Fox's dad did. He rolled up his sleeve, lifted the cow's tail, and literally thrust his arm up its asshole, past the elbow even, digging around in there for the magnet. He even put his cheek on the cow's rump, so he could concentrate on finding it. I could tell he was worried. That cow meant a lot of expense.

What I noticed most was Fox's reaction when his dad did this. It brought an intense look of disgust and rage to Fox's face. I could see all sorts of ideas connecting up in his head about its significance, some of them reasonable and others not, but none very appealing in what they suggested about life on a ranch. Right then he hated that cow, he hated his dad, he hated the whole world. And he hated the fact that Zach and I were witnesses. "Come on," he said, walking away, but we lingered despite ourselves, to see if his dad would find the magnet. Fox lunged back and jerked us both toward him. "Come the fuck on, dickheads!"

As I said before, life could feel like a trap in Mendocino for some of my friends. They had a difficult time imagining themselves outside the choices their parents had made. Zach wasn't college material either. He did have one definite skill: selling marijuana He'd been doing it for years, with swash-buckling brio, as he had to rip it off from various growers he'd spy on all through the summer. He would follow them out to their patches and keep track of their daily routines until it came time to harvest. This often made for adventure. Zach was always trespassing.

However, selling pot was also a problem for him, as it was for many people who did that sort of thing in Mendocino. It accustomed him to a lifestyle he couldn't afford any other way, and he had to live in constant fear of getting caught by growers or by drug enforcement agents. He also had to lie about what he did to almost everybody around him, and that's harder to do than you might think. It limited him more and more to the society of those for whom it wouldn't matter what laws he broke. It roped him, in other words, more tightly into a hillbilly life he hated just as much as Fox hated his ranch.

For Zach it may have been more frightening on account of his parents. They used to be environmental activists who drove spikes into trees and occupied redwood groves slated for harvest. But Zach told me they'd been exposed to lead some years back, and now it made them so tired they pretty much had to sleep all day. They'd even set up their beds in the living room of their rundown house to make it easier, getting up only to eat or go to the bathroom. I'd never seen two more lethargic people in my life.

Zach blamed his parents' condition on the FBI, which had poisoned them, he claimed, as punishment for their militant resistance to the logging companies. I didn't know whether to believe that or not. Someone broke into their house, anyway, and scattered lead shavings all over the place. By the time his parents found out about it, the damage had been done. It was another reason why Zach sold marijuana, and why he'd most likely take the next step after high school of becoming a grower himself: his parents needed his help just to get by. I never heard him complain about the pressure that put on him, but it was obviously another spring in the trap.

And if Zach seemed a measure of how finely grained the woodwork could get in Mendocino, or how remote one of its high school kids might be from a consideration as simple as going to college, I couldn't even begin to describe Cooper. As I've said, his life was a total blank.

My mother kept me from thinking about college. Ever since I could remember she was always getting sick. I assumed the fatigue and shortness of breath she complained about were due to cigarettes, which she basically smoked one right after another. But I never thought she had a serious problem until easy things, like carrying a bag of dog food from the van or lifting animals into cages, started getting harder for her to do. When I was fifteen, a doctor ran some tests and discovered tissue damage to the alveolar walls in her lungs. That meant emphysema, a congenital disease for which there was no known cure.

The news devastated my mother, as she now had to face up to drastic changes, and they proved next to impossible to make. She couldn't quit smoking no matter how much she tried or I shamed her into it. She'd sneak out to the liquor store in town for another pack, or she'd hide them around the house where she could get at them in a pinch. I was always ferreting them out of cupboards and tin cans under beds.

She also hated doctors. "I don't go to hospitals," she regularly declared. "Hospitals are dangerous places." She took pride in her self-reliance; like a settler on some frontier, she preferred to deal with things on her own. I think it was the break down of this capacity for independence that bothered her the most. In fact it terrified her, because it meant she had to rely on others in a manner that experience had taught her led to disaster. She didn't trust people when it came down to it. She liked them when she didn't need anything from them. That way she didn't have to worry about their hidden stores of anger or hate, the wolf's head that leapt out of perfectly good-natured faces when you least expected it, or most counted on their decency. It was better to take everyone at face value but assume the worst in their heart of hearts, and she only knew how to do this when anything she might need was a function of her own ability to get it, make it, grow it, or tend it.

I could hardly consider going off to college under these circumstances. I'd thought about applying to Sonoma State, since it was only a couple hours' drive away and close enough for me still to come and help her out. But the truth was it wouldn't be long before she needed me for even basic things. There'd be no question of her running the kennel by herself even in a year or two. By then she'd need more than the masks and pills the doctors had her using. She'd have to carry around an oxygen tank, which meant, among other things, quitting cigarettes for good, and I didn't see how she could on her own. So I felt roped in myself to staying around Mendocino after high school. Not that it was a question in my mind, even for a second; I was going to take care of my mother for as long as she needed me. No one else would if I didn't.

I worried plenty about the rest of my life, though. The fear stabbed right down into my dreams, keeping me up at night the way emphysema could my mother. I don't mean I felt as suffocated as she did, afraid of not ever being able to breathe again, but it worked on the breath all the same to wonder how I was going to live and meet the needs I'd have for livelihood, friendship, love. It added a whole other dimension to those confabulations with myself down at the catch pond or on Point Cabrillo by the lighthouse, where I'd go to watch the swallows dart out of their nests under the eaves and rise with the afternoon light, catching bugs to eat.

Not all those walks on the Point were so burdened by worry. Sometimes they helped me to sort out my feelings, gain perspective, and get clearer about things. On occasion they even afforded new clues and resources I might not have found anywhere else.

One day, for instance, I happened to be sitting in the grass with four dogs, all happy as clams after the long descent through the headland, when all at once they leapt up and started barking at Chase's father coming to a halt at a nearby bluff. He was looking through a pair of binoculars out to sea. In the full light of day he seemed even older than I thought, maybe sixty, although he had the same solid frame as his son and the same assured way of holding himself. I even fancied for a moment that he was a phantom Chase stepping out from the future.

The dogs rushed off, barking a little too fiercely and disturbing the man's concentration. I swung upright and called out their names. This quieted them down, and I tentatively approached. "Sorry about that."

"No problem," he answered.

I gazed out to sea in the direction where he was looking so intently. I didn't notice anything right away, only whitecaps teeming to the horizon, but then several whales simultaneously creased the swell with their humps and spouted. They weren't more than a quarter of a mile off.

"It's early for gray whales," I remarked.

"They're not gray whales," he said. "They're great blues, a whole pod of them." He handed me the binoculars. "Here."

I focused on what appeared to be seven or eight whales now, so resolved in the ground glass that I could see the mottled discolorations of their skin.

"What are they doing?"

"Probably feeding on the plankton beds."

"I've never seen them here before."

"Blue whales don't have a recognizable territory or migration pattern—none we've been able to establish anyway. They range pretty much through all the oceans."

"Huh," I said, impressed.

"They make the loudest sound in nature under that water. It might even be as loud as the most intense man-made explosions—short of an atomic bomb. That's how they're able to range so far. Their signals travel hundreds of miles. When you combine that with the networks of different pods like this one, all bouncing information off each other, it makes more sense that the whole ocean would be their territory."

There was a marked reticence in his voice. It came from down in his throat and seemed oddly formal. It carried authority in a way I don't think I'd ever heard before.

"Right now, they might know what's happening off the coast of Tasmania," he added.

The thought deserved more wonder than he gave it, from which I inferred a long practical experience that might have left him a little jaded. But it still heartened me to see him appreciate something I did, too, in those communicating networks of pods: a complexity in the natural world that worked as well upon our human nature, puzzling the will. It suggested a scruple I recognized in Chase's dad as a sense of vocation, a calling. And for maybe the first time I found myself asking if it wasn't my own potential for this calling that kept me returning to the Point—not from fear or to hide away, but for the sake of a commitment I wanted obscurely to be making. There was energy in aversion, as I've also said before, and it comforted me to feel that all it might need to come out was the right kind of trust and encouragement.

Not that I got much of either from Chase's dad. After I handed back the binoculars, he resumed his study of the blue whales and more or less forgot I was there. That threw me a little. It made me question how much we had in common after all. Just because I sensed in him qualities I could relate to didn't mean they were the qualities that made him worldly, or that his worldliness rubbed off on me. I was only sensing a part of his life—not the part, for instance, that he shared with the glamorous woman I spied on in my computer. That was a feat bordering on the miraculous to my mind. She didn't seem like someone I could know, let alone love or live with on a daily basis.

I tried to imagine them as husband and wife. Chase's dad was obviously handsome, even for a man his age. They were matched in that respect. But otherwise, I couldn't see much similarity between them. Where he had steadiness of purpose and an inner life, with its own coordinates of concern and obligation, she existed outside herself, or in the eyes of others; all those fantasies she acted out told you nothing about her and everything about the people who saw them.

I suppose she took satisfaction in that. Modeling was, after all, a career for her. But still, I couldn't fit this man's privacy together in my mind with her publicness. Maybe they didn't fit. Or, more perplexing still, they did fit, all too well in fact, each a kind of self-absorption, a species of detachment, and that was how the two of them got on with each other, in separate spheres, on parallel tracks. Maybe that was also why things ended in tragedy.

On my way back home that day, I saw my neighbor Miriam standing in the little flourishing garden she'd made next to her trailer. She waved me over to her chicken wire fence, and we chatted in the sign language I'd learned, which pleased her to no end. She smiled back at me from under her floppy hat, then ran inside to get the pad of paper she used to write on. She seemed eager for me to linger.

Miriam was a lonely woman. She didn't have many friends, and there didn't seem to be much affection between her and her husband. He was a gruff and solemn man who didn't welcome conversation. I hardly ever saw them together. He tended to lurk in the house when I came around, or sit in an old Bentwood rocking chair on the other side of the garden and read. I think he resented the fact that his wife was deaf.

She hadn't always been that way. She told me she'd experienced a temporary loss of hearing as a child after a case of measles, but the problem recurred in her teens, and from then on it slowly worsened. She could still remember what it was like to talk with people, although now she preferred not to because she'd lost her confidence with it. It shamed her to imagine what other people heard when she opened her mouth.

She came back out scribbling furiously on her pad, then tore off the sheet and handed it to me with a theatrical flourish, like a servant delivering a letter to a king. Miriam had a sense of humor for all that was lacking in her life. The note said: *You're a dryad of the woods!*

That struck me as a little odd. She had eccentric tastes, gleaned, I suspect, from the books she liked to read as much as her husband did. She often said things that came out of left field like that. But I had an idea of what she meant. The walk through the headlands had left me sun-shot and blowsy.

She knelt down to pet the dogs, which had gathered for the attention. When she'd finished with them, she reached up and touched the brim of my buffalo hide hat, letting me know she approved. I guess she hadn't seen it before.

"A friend gave it to me," I told her. She watched my lips, wondering a little too long about my friend.

Then she wrote in her pad: *She knows exactly what looks good on you!*

That made me blush. To hide my embarrassment, I hurried to tell her about the blue whales and what I'd learned about them from Chase's dad.

I wish I could have been there.

"I'd go back down with you, but they've probably moved on by now."

She shrugged, her gaze shifting to two Monterey pines that stood next to her trailer, just inside the borders of the preserve. They'd turned wan and gray like so many on the coast, because of a beetle infestation. I saw resin dripped down the bole, too, which indicated some kind of pitch canker.

They used to be so green.

"You'll have to cut them down."

They look like ghosts.

To banish this thought from her mind, she turned to the garden, which gave her the idea of picking tomatoes for me to take home. She gathered some in a grocery bag and handed them over.

"You sure you don't want them?"

There's too many for just me. They'll spoil.

"Where's Daniel?"

She arched a mischievous eyebrow, like a suspect in a murder mystery. I wasn't sure whether she knew or not. But she grabbed me lightly at the elbow and drew me into the grassy open area, pointing down the headland to the sea. On the far side of the lighthouse I saw a fishing boat at a tide line, all rods up.

She gave me her pad. *He stays out there sometimes for days at a time.* I detected no special disappointment in this fact. Indeed, I had a feeling she preferred him to be gone. That made me a little sad. It reminded me one more time of Chase's mom and dad, and of the steps we take to protect ourselves from the pain of living.

6

Practice began soon after that, scheduled five days a week with two a day on Saturday. From then on we might as well have been in boot camp. No lapse of discipline was permitted, and if you coasted any part of the time Coach had you in his charge, he dressed you down to an edge of abuse that outsiders would be shocked to hear. I suspect he made the gym off-limits to the public while we were in it to avoid this possibility. Some parents, and even teachers, had complained over the years about his style being inappropriate for high school.

But we understood why he went too far like that, even when it bordered on the downright mean. Coach had a temper that could detonate. Sometimes he didn't even pretend to control it. It seemed to be a point of honor with him; it connected in his mind with some deep rebellion against the world. He had little respect for rules. His was a jealous God, an outsider God of the wilderness or the desert. We liked this about him. As fearsome as he might be, it meant he thought of you as an equal in one respect: this volatility, this flaming out of a desire that lacked any trace of indifference or hypocrisy whatever else might be true. Coach was nothing if not *personal*, and if the price to pay for that had to be his excesses, then we couldn't exactly hate him for them without hating his personality, too, or calling it to account in the name of rules we didn't particularly respect either. That would involve something like snitching—the worst thing you could do in Coach's book. He wanted us to think of ourselves as less a team than a gang, bound together by secret rites and oaths of blood.

Coach's system had us pushing the envelop of convention even on the floor. The idea was to run our opponent ragged. There should be no pauses in the general onslaught of full-court pressure, both on offense and defense. He wanted us to open the game up as widely as possible to the unforeseen and the accidental. We had to run on instinct all the time.

Still, a calculus applied to the forces we set in motion this way: man-to-man defense, filling lanes on fast breaks, perpetual picking and rolling. The idea was to attack the basket, take your man on, and force mismatches that could be exploited: a little guy on a big guy, a slow guy on a fast guy. And if it happened the other way around, you worked hard to double-team or switch back as fast as you could. I called it the playground style on steroids. It worked best when you felt as supple and easy in it as you would playing at the middle school on a summer's day. Coach often put it that way, in fact.

The most important thing for a game of this sort was stamina, and toward that end Coach ran us to exhaustion every day. One particularly grueling drill was full-court three-on-twos, which he'd keep us going at for what could seem like forever. We kept going, literally, until somebody threw up on the sidelines. Quickly enough we stopped looking forward to practice because of this.

We were all pretty resilient, though, because we'd gotten used to Coach's style the year before. Only Chase had some adjustments to make. He came in blind to the drama Coach staged and the tolerance it required. He could bristle when he felt heat directed at him. Of course, he was also the purest athlete on the court and the best suited for Coach's kind of game. He was quicker than any of us, mostly because of his footwork I noticed, which was very sure and precise. It allowed for sharp shifts of gravity that often left us wondering how he got from one point to another. He moved around a lot, too, keeping his opponent off balance. You had to be aware around Chase, since any lapse or slip was enough for him to take advantage of it. And the worst, or the best, part was it all seemed so natural, a simple extension of his physical prowess, and not the result of any strategy.

Chase could also leap higher than anybody I'd ever seen. Even Fox, who was 6'5" and built like a tank, had to have a running start to dunk the ball. But Chase could put his elbows over the rim just standing there, and he knew how to hang in the air for what seemed like an impossible length of time.

Coach added plays that exploited this capability. I had a lot to do with them since I was the point guard, the one who, more than anybody, had to keep the ever-shifting patterns of the game in mind. One of these plays required that I loft the ball close enough to the basket for Chase to come slashing off a pick, grab it in mid-air, and hammer it into the basket. I'd never seen anyone do that the way he could. It reminded me of a move an NBA player might make.

On occasion practices could spill over into outright violence. Especially when Coach singled people out for attack, we almost couldn't stand the pressure. At some level I wondered if he didn't want us to hate him, since he pushed us sometimes right up to the point of lashing out. No one dared lash out, of course, because we had little reason to think he wouldn't hit back.

One night about two weeks after the first practice, Zach was the guy who couldn't do anything right. We were working on the architecture of the full-court press and Zach kept missing his mark at the center of the floor, where the ball ended up in the hands of the one guy who could break the press right apart. Each time this happened the growl in Coach's voice grew deeper until, finally, he walked straight into the drill, grabbed Zach by his jersey, and flung him across the floor. He fell, sliding in his own sweat, to the place he was supposed to be.

Zach had the most attitude of any guy on the team. He could court disaster without thinking twice about the consequences. I had the feeling he'd grown up fighting superior powers with all the doomed recklessness of Custer on his last stand. In this spirit he muttered from the floor, "Cocksucker."

Coach reacted with a startling velocity. He lifted Zach up with both hands and held him in close to his body.

"What did you say?"

"I said, 'Sorry, sir.'"

"The hell you did," Coach said, shoving him back again to the floor. Then he gave Zach a savage kick in the back. "Don't you *ever* talk to me that way."

He would have kicked him again if Fox and Chase hadn't gotten between them and stared Coach down. In that moment I don't think he knew what he would do. He looked hard from one to the other and then at the rest of us, who (with the exception of Jordi) surged just perceptibly forward to show we all agreed he needed to back off. Coach went oddly blank then. His eyes seemed to open into a well of darkness that had no touchable bottom. All I did catch there was the flash of a world of pain far more terrifying than anything I had maybe ever seen in another person.

"It's not fair," Chase quietly asserted, because he knew he might have been the only one there who could.

"Who ever said things were fair?" Coach countered from inside that well.

"We're all trying our best."

Coach nodded as if nothing could be less true, but the tension through his shoulders relaxed. The hand on his hip went limp, and his defiantly crooked elbow sank by his side. You could feel him grappling with the shame that had to be overcome before backing down was possible. You could also feel him giving up, either on us or on the situation. He stared off toward the front entrance. Then he said, "I'll be back when you guys are ready to be men," and walked straight out of the gym.

We stood flat-footed and watched him go. "What was that about?" Chase demanded after a beat. Only I understood he meant the pain in Coach's eyes.

"He's hot-headed," said Fox.

"He was out of line."

"Everyone gets mad sometimes." I could see Fox was thinking of himself when he said this. I felt the winds suddenly shift.

"Not everyone's a coach."

"I don't care what he is."

"You would if it was you on the floor right now."

That had the effect of cornering Fox in his contradictions, which he didn't like at all. His eyes started to dart.

"If he treated me that way," Chase went on obliviously, "I'd sue his damn ass."

Fox erupted. "Shut up!" he cried, shoving him.

Now I had to step between them.

Jarred, but not exactly surprised by Fox's outburst, Chase said, "What the fuck's your problem?"

"You're my problem!" Fox bellowed right through me. "You fucking rich ass piece of shit."

"Stop it," I said. "Come on, Fox. We don't need to fight."

At that instant Jordi blurted out, "*Just win!*" This rattled everybody. We turned and saw him standing off to the side, big earnest tears glistening in his eyes. Our attention broke the confidence with which he spoke. "Just win and it'll be all right," he stammered. "We just have to keep winning."

His words confused us, if only because we had no idea what to make of his odd pleading tone. Or maybe that wasn't true. There was an explanation. It had gone unspoken by all of us since practice first started: the likelihood that Chase's presence in our midst meant Jordi would lose his spot on the starting team. That was another reason why he was crying anyway.

Chase gave me a ride home afterward. He couldn't get over what had happened as we drove through the night up Highway 1 toward Point Cabrillo. "You guys are too intense," he said.

"We get pretty wound up sometimes."

"It's just a game." I sensed him drawing on his other world of experience. "It doesn't matter—at least not the way you all think it does."

A little defensively myself I said, "There's a lot going on under the surface."

"You've got to keep your cool," Chase went on. "Everybody who's good at the game knows that."

I waited for him to say more.

"It's what you admire about them," he said. "They internalize the rules. The game becomes second nature to them, like breathing." He broke off, dissatisfied with the analogy.

"That makes sense," I said, urging him on.

"You don't let things boil over like that. It gives others too much power. Coach understands this. He's always driving at it when he lectures us. But he sure as shit doesn't hold himself back."

"Maybe he can't."

"But you've got to, Woody, because I'm telling you, in this world, you're dead if you don't."

I felt the conviction in that on the many levels Chase meant it. We drove without speaking, both of us thinking about Coach and his raw anger.

"That guy has a dark side," Chase said presently. "Crazy dark. I've never seen anything like it."

"Maybe that's because you don't know people like him," I said with too much sharpness. I wanted *my* experience to count for something here, too.

"What do you mean?" He wondered at my tone, but he also didn't dismiss the feeling in it out of hand.

"I mean he comes from a place you don't know," I said. "You take things for granted he can't."

"Like what?"

I shrugged, half because I thought it was clear and half because I still couldn't say just what Chase took for granted. He sensed more in my silence than the answer it implied.

"What is it you see in that guy?" he asked then. "I really don't get it, Woody. So what if he's had a rough life? So what if he comes from the wrong side of the tracks? He's still a total asshole." He stared through the windshield. "A real bar fucker."

That word struck a nerve so tender I had no ready response. Chase could make me feel very exposed, as if he saw right through me. All I could think was that I probably didn't come from a place he knew either, but he guessed that thought in me, too.

"It's a father thing, isn't it?" he said. "You miss that authority in your life." He glanced at me to see if I had taken offense. "Maybe I'm wrong."

"No. I'm thinking about it."

"I *hate* my father," he declared, gearing the BMW down on the approach to the turnoff for Cabrillo Drive. "That's the difference between us, Woody. I can't stand to be around him. He's been pushing me so hard for so long I about cracked up. Now he knows better than to show any interest in what I do."

"Why?"

"Because the minute he does, I won't do it anymore."

As I've said, I never knew my father. My mother could be positively cryptic when she talked about him, but one word she had used to describe him was "bar fucker," so I could hardly object to Chase's guess at my attitude toward Coach. I suppose he was a father figure to me, however much it crossed up my sympathies to make him one. I did, on some level, excuse his faults when they didn't match my own sense of right and wrong. Why I did that touched on the knotted feelings of a son whose mother had once been physically abused by a man. I took her side in every way, with every fiber of my being, but I was a man, too, and there was something so absolute about that abuse in her mind that it left me no other place to stand than in the shoes of the abuser. All I could do was take responsibility for it, see it, feel it, guard against it in myself. It wasn't, then, that I excused Coach's faults as that I wanted him to be a better man than he had been. I wanted him to show me that it was possible to be this better man. That was the more ardent source of my allegiance to him.

These thoughts took a new twist for me the very next day, when Coop, Zach, and I bought our lunches at a market in town and went to a small beach off the headlands. We sat on driftwood logs and looked out over the water with the hoods of our varsity sweatshirts pulled up against the cold. Zach lit a fat joint before he started eating. "If I can't block out the world with my mind," he said, thinking we needed an excuse for this breach of discipline, "I'd go completely nuts."

Coop, staring at the crisply snapping waves on the beach, flashed the weird smile that was as near to expressive as he often ever got, thinking of last night's practice. "How's your back?" he asked dryly.

"This shit works as a painkiller, too," Zach said.

I suggested that he better be ready for practice that evening.

"Don't worry. I'm over it. Yesterday was a fluke. I couldn't concentrate."

"It's hard, keeping everything in mind at once," I said.

"Maybe I should play stoned."

"I don't think that's a good idea."

"It could help my shot," he went on. "I concentrate more when I'm high. Things get very clear and connected."

"You're a good shooter without pot," I assured him, absorbed in the approach up the beach of a woman with silver hair cut short like a man's. Her hands were dug deep in the pockets of a navy blue pea coat. She seemed unusually distracted, too susceptible to the long dream of the cormorant's flight over the water or the wood chimes that dangled in the throat of a hovering crow.

"I'm all right," said Zach. "I'm hot and I'm cold. I can't control it. Somebody else is turning the faucet on and off." He followed my eyes to the strange woman, noticing her fitful progress. "Story of my life, man."

Coop leaned toward us. "You know who that is?" he whispered.

"No," we said.

"Jordi's mom."

Before I could protest, the woman came within earshot. At that point I saw what bothered me about her. She was talking to herself, just under her breath. She was trying to be discreet, but it was still an undeniable mutter. I sensed she'd been wandering around like that for a long time, in her own world. I don't think she even knew we were there.

When she'd passed I said, "That's not Jordi's mom."

Coop nodded. "He told me himself. She's his *real* mom."

Jordi had never said anything about that to me. I'd always assumed Anastasia was his real mom. I wondered why it had never come up, or if there had been signs and I'd missed them somehow. We watched her angle toward the stairs that led up the cliff face and over a sea cave to the headland, still lost her thoughts.

"That's what you get for marrying a cocksucker like Coach," Zach cracked, unable to stop himself.

Her name was Terry. She'd moved to Mendocino only a month before and rented a saltbox house two blocks from the middle school. I learned this from my mother, who met Terry by chance at the bar in the Mendocino Hotel about a week later. I found them one night after practice, deep in conversation over Irish coffees and smoking like chimneys. Unsurprisingly, they'd hit it off right away.

My mother introduced her as "Coach's ex," and I shook her hand, looking in her eyes for some hint of that same distraction I saw on the beach. It didn't seem to be there now.

"You're a friend of Jordi's?" she asked.

"I've known him a long time, yeah."

"Wish I could say the same. I don't know him at all." Her sadness as she said this was unmistakable. "I'm like a stranger to him."

I had no idea what to say to this avowal, and my mother watched us both with compressed lips, not letting anything on, as was her way. She was nothing if not discreet. A moment later Terry changed the subject.

My mother knew a lot, though, since Terry had just finished telling the whole story of her life with Coach. As I found out afterward, they'd known each other from before he played basketball at the University of Oklahoma. They'd both grown up in farm towns and had the same legacies of poverty and precarity to deal with later in life. The experience left Coach scarily self-assured on the outside, but just as scarily unstable on the inside. Because Terry understood this better than anyone else, she helped to balance the pressures building up in him as it began to look like basketball could turn into a professional career. He needed her measure as a check on his volatile side.

They got married in his final year of college. But then he received the letter drafting him into the Army, and he had to choose between showing up at the induction center or escaping to Canada, which would mean never being able to play again as a draft dodger.

He came back from Vietnam even more troubled than before. He was angry and bitter because he wasn't the player he used to be. After failing to get on with any NBA teams, he settled for a semi-professional career in South America and, ironically, Canada, playing in largely vacant arenas on mediocre teams.

Terry followed him through the grueling seasons of travel from city to city, encouraging him in the break away from that gravitational pull of his past. It still held him, though, and he increasingly turned to whiskey as a means of bearing up under it. When he started losing his edge as a player, and it became apparent that he'd have to give up on his dream altogether, he took to drinking more heavily.

His relation to Terry deteriorated at the same time. Where before he'd counted on her as a touchstone, a link to an earlier sense of accomplishment, now he began to blame her for his failures. The more she tried to help him, the more her help became the problem, the reminder, the weight of a disappointed life. He started assistant coaching, and their vagabonding continued in the same fitful way. But a downward spiral had set in that would only worsen as he went on undermining himself. He couldn't keep any job for long, and his first as a head coach, in Edmonton, was also his last. It ended after one season of dismal losing that pushed him right up to the edge of nervous collapse.

They returned to the US, where he started a job as a high school coach in Redding. By then he had no mastery over his impulses, and his treatment of Terry turned into physical abuse. She told my mother she'd spent a lot of time making excuses for him, holding fast in the violence to a memory of the man that she had a harder and harder time separating from wish or prayer. She was strong-willed, accustomed since her own childhood to adversity, but the effort slid like a sinking ship into depths of self-deception as livid as the bruises she only knew how to ignore. In a way that I could see on that beach still marked her all these years later, Terry began to live like a woman underwater, without breath or light, far removed from either aid or comfort.

Unfortunately, her glassy distance made her husband feel all the more abandoned. On the day the high school where he'd been coaching fired him for one of his rages, he came home and beat her into unconsciousness. The only witness, she said, was Jordi, five years old at the time, standing in a corner of the room, terrified.

7

I couldn't get that image of Jordi out of my mind afterward. It worried all my ideas about Coach, about basketball, about just what we were doing there on that court during those practices. I still wanted to believe the game held out some hope of a change in what it meant to be a man, but it was less clear to me now that I'd properly separated this desire from the men we were becoming, let alone the man Coach was. I wondered how far he might go in his anger before judgment cut out.

I also wondered how far I might go looking the other way. The stakes were high, after all. High enough to bend whole lives permanently out of shape. Was I really taking responsibility for that anger, or was I siding with it, enabling it even? Not only out there in others, but in myself as well? It was getting more difficult for me to know, at any rate, just how far off my scruples and qualms might have been from simple excuses.

Hardest to deal with was Jordi, whose adjustment to being second string I saw now in a different light. His dad showed him no mercy, even going out of his way to rub the humiliation in. His role in practice was often to help refine the systems of offense and defense, almost as if he were an assistant coach. It felt worse than unfair. It felt as if he was punishing Jordi for his own mistakes.

Jordi took it all stoically, like any tried and true son of an abused woman might have. In my new understanding of the situation, I could see him thinking that as long as the anger was directed at him, it wouldn't be directed elsewhere. I'd probably have thought the same thing, to be honest. But the burden of it was also wearing him down.

This drama between father and son made the first preseason game uncomfortable, particularly the first time we went out onto the floor while Jordi sat on the bench and proceeded to watch. It got no better when we pulled ahead of the other team, and Coach began substituting for the starters. Then it became doubly humiliating for Jordi, as we had no choice but to watch him with the scrubs make the game closer than it otherwise would have been.

⁂

Things were getting more complicated for me on other fronts, too. My mother's health was deteriorating. One night she had a bad night of coughing, and by dawn she was hungry enough for air to think she needed an infusion of oxygen the doctors sometimes gave her. I drove her in our van to the hospital in Fort Bragg, where she had to be later that day for some tests anyway. I decided to stay home from school and wait with her until the appointment.

We passed Ryder striding in his ubiquitous checked jacket on the side of the road. I didn't see him make any hitchhiker's signs and so assumed he wasn't looking for a ride, but just as we swung by I noticed him holding his left hand tightly with a blood-stained towel. I slammed on the brakes, rattling my mother, and pulled over.

Walking back down the shoulder I called out, "You all right?"

He pulled the towel back enough to show me a gash between his thumb and forefinger. "Gotta get to the hospital," he said, stating the obvious.

I offered to take him. "We're headed there ourselves."

At the van I slid the side door open for him to get in. My mother craned her neck to take a look. "That's a nasty cut, Ryder," she remarked in that deadpan style of hers.

"B-broken bottle," he stuttered. He did that when he was rattled. "Nearly s-s-sliced my thumb off."

"Looks like you could use some stitches."

He didn't answer, just attended to the wound as a rank seaweed odor filled the cab. Who knew where he'd been sleeping that night.

At the clinic they gave my mother the oxygen infusion and a spirometry test, which showed still more degeneration in her lungs. The doctor said her case bordered on severe and that if she didn't knuckle down and make some changes, she risked things like kidney damage or outright respiratory failure.

My mother listened, her indomitable spirit collapsing a little more as she grappled with the paradox of yielding her will to live in order to live. She still wasn't ready to accept that. The doctor prescribed a new inhaler and some antibiotics, which my mother might or might not take.

"It's the damn steroids that cause the kidney damage in the first place," she complained as we sat waiting for the prescriptions afterward.

"You have no choice, Mom."

"There's the herbal remedies," she said doubtfully.

We both knew they didn't work.

She fell into brooding reflection. "I won't be dependent on them," she declared presently. "I won't be one of their ghouls." She looked at me askance to see how I'd take that. She mistook my silence for encouragement. "I'd rather check out nice and easy, while I've still got my self-respect."

I pretended not to take that seriously, but behind the fear it roused in me, I knew she probably meant it. I don't think we'd ever touched so closely on the possibility that she might die, and neither of us were up to talking it out. I did think of something to ask her, though. Something more tangential, if still crossing one of her tacit boundaries. "Would it have been easier for you," I asked, "if things had been different with dad?"

I wasn't comfortable saying that word. He'd never been my dad. But it didn't sound right calling him by his name either. Billy. Billy Thompson.

"You mean quitting cigarettes?"

"Or even getting sick. Would you have started on them, gotten so hooked, if he hadn't been the man he was?"

She could tell these questions weighed on me more than usual right then, so she let me touch on the tender spot my father was for her. "Who knows, Woody. You can't go through life blaming others for your mistakes. We can't control what happens to us, but I think we do have some leeway when it comes to how we respond. I don't blame him for that. And I don't regret much either, to tell the truth. Lots of good things come from disaster. You, for instance! You're the one good thing Billy managed to accomplish."

"Am I like him?" I meant not so much in looks, since I knew there was a resemblance, but on more emotional levels.

"No, Woody," she said, shaking her head. "You're nothing like him."

"Not even when he was young, before he got so mean?"

"There was no before. He was always a sonofabitch."

The nurse behind the counter called out her name, and she went to pick up her meds, glad to change the subject. When she came back, I suggested we get breakfast at a diner in Fort Bragg. The doctor said she had to eat more protein. As we talked that over, Ryder appeared in the waiting room. He'd gotten stitches. The bandage looked like a boxing glove.

"Better?" I asked.

He nodded.

"At least it's not your shooting hand."

He hardly heard me. His experience inside the clinic had spooked him. In fact he was so antsy to leave that he started walking off toward the door without another word.

"Hey, Ryder!" I called after him. "Come have breakfast with us!"

With a backward wave he said, "Out of here!"

"It's our treat!"

"O-on my way!"

"Hey!" I almost shouted. "It's basketball season, you know!" This had been a little ritual of ours for years now. I asked him to come see us play, and he never did.

By the door he paused long enough to finish with a wave and a slowly parsed, "Sa-yo-na-ra!" Then he was gone.

We stood before the empty vestibule. "He hates hospitals, too," my mother quipped.

❦

Those early weeks of practice coincided with the first appearance of gray whales off the coast. I saw them from Point Cabrillo the Sunday after that trip to the hospital. I'd walked four dogs through the preserve and sat for a while at the cliff's edge when three of them surfaced just on the other side of the surf line. They blew water into diaphanous sheen and lingered at the sheeted surface for air, taking four or five breaths in twenty-second intervals, a pattern they repeated all the way through their journey without variation. It wasn't the only pattern they held to so consistently either. I knew, for instance, that they hardly ate, straining their invertebrate prey in baleen during the months they spent in the Bering Straits and pretty much fasting all the way to their breeding grounds in Baja. Gray whales were very self-contained creatures in my mind. I used to think of them when I was a kid not as traveling between Alaska and Mexico but as moving in place, like one of those streaming digital signs. They carried the whole ocean in their serene lidded eyes and on their scored and grooved skin. They were *part of* the ocean more than *in* it, denser nodes of a single living and breathing ecosystem.

I would find out how true this was that same day. Heading back home a while later, I met Suzanne driving her mother's station wagon along the main road of the preserve. She stopped and rolled down the window.

"Want to hear whale songs?" she asked.

"Yes," I promptly replied. As usual her voice and presence elated me. I leaned in to catch her scent: sage. I noticed a red silk rose sewn into the embroidered yoke of the black dress she was wearing, laid over the modest swell of her breasts.

I was disappointed to find out what, of course, I knew already. Chase had invited her to his father's sound studio. But I opened the hatch anyway, shunted the dogs inside, and drove with her back to the compound by the lighthouse.

I asked her how things were going in as casual a tone as I could muster, but she guessed what was on my mind.

"You mean with Chase?"

"Sure," I said. "If you want to tell me."

She thought about it. "I don't know. He's elusive sometimes."

"How so?"

"It's hard to tell what he's feeling."

"He keeps you guessing, eh?" It was all I could think to say.

"Maybe. Or he just doesn't like me that much."

"He likes you," I returned, not quite having it in me to add what he'd said at Deadman's.

"You think so?"

I stared straight ahead through the windshield, trying not to frown. It was clear her heart leapt at the prospect. "Seems that way to me," I said at last.

I might have revealed in that too much of how I really felt. As she stopped the car by the compound and pulled the handbrake, she gave me a searching look.

"What do you know?" she asked, in a bantering tone.

"Plenty!"

"Like what?"

I wanted to say, *What any jealous man knows*, but I refrained. Mercifully, I was rescued by one of the dogs. It had jumped seats from the back and begun licking my neck, right below the ear. That distracted us both enough to forget the conversation.

Chase and his father hadn't done much with the house where they lived. The furniture wasn't theirs, nor the pans in the kitchen, the plates, the cutlery. It felt more temporary than I'd be comfortable with for a whole year. I could tell it irritated Chase. He said his dad was the type of man who could live in a concrete bunker and not care. It's where he was in his mind that mattered. Just so long as he could do his physics, Chase said.

He took us into an office crammed with computers and other electronic equipment. We found his dad behind a desk covered with books, manuals, policy reports, and what looked like seismographic charts and graphs. He greeted us with that voice back in his throat and a formality of diction that just missed being cold. But he seemed to be in a gregarious enough mood as he explained to us what he did, which was "model the energetics of marine mammals in their natural environment."

It wasn't obvious at first what this meant. I learned then a fact that common sense would have been enough to figure out, and yet it had never occurred to me before: that the ocean, under normally turbid conditions, is more or less pitch black, and whales can hardly see their own flukes even in surface light. Sound is their equivalent to sight. After cetaceans decided they'd had enough of the land and returned to the sea some fifty million years ago, they evolved, in the conch-shaped spiral of their inner ears, features that could read a spectrum of sounds largely inaudible to us. Different whales lived at different frequencies, Chase's dad said, or rather they lived *in* different frequencies. What he seemed to do, in other words, was understand sound in terms of space and architecture.

He went on to talk about biology and soundscapes as if they were the same thing. In this way of thinking, whales didn't just use hums and clicks to hone in on fish; fish were intrinsically hums and clicks. They didn't so much find mates through sound as mate sonically. Pups and calves, he said, resonate with their mothers more than they bond or love.

I formed a clear picture of how his mind worked listening to him explain all this, and it made him a lot more interesting than he might have seemed on the surface. A depth opened up in his words that could be dizzying to plumb. Suzanne was in free fall already. Of course, a quick glance at Chase showed there might not have been as much below that surface in his dad as that. Only another kind of darkness. I could tell by the frown on Chase's face that he wasn't as impressed as we were, and half regretted having arranged for us to come.

After a while his dad played recordings of different whales' songs. He explained that the humpback produced compositions "as complex as a concerto," with phrases and themes that were continually developed and modified. The blue whale produced these loud moans or booms that made you think of earthquakes in the ocean floor. The fin whale emitted long strings of regular pulses that traveled hundreds of miles through the more ductile channels of sound in the ocean. To my ear they resembled the creaking of timber in tall ships. You had the impression that the ocean was an echo chamber of these sounds.

Chase's dad followed this with songs of actual gray whales, which were monitored through a sonobuoy that had been dropped offshore for this purpose. They were murkier, harder to distinguish from the general drone of the water. Suzanne heard more in them than mere noise.

"That sounds like a propeller," she said.

"It probably is," said Chase's dad. "You can hear a super-tanker coming a day before it arrives. There's a lot of man-made noise out there."

"How much?"

"Well, more and more. It's difficult to measure."

"Enough to make it hard for the whales to pick up their own songs?"

"There's definitely an upward trend in the distortion."

Chase shifted on his feet. He now seemed more uncom-fortable than bored. I had the feeling it bothered him to see his girlfriend question his dad so directly. He was eager to leave.

Suzanne appeared to miss this unease in him. "What else makes noise?" she asked.

"All sorts of things," his father replied. "Ship traffic, commercial sonar, oil drilling platforms, the harassment devices that fishermen use, tunnel borers, transmitters. Even jet skis and powerboats."

"That seems like a lot."

"It can be."

"And you study that, too—the 'upward trend'?"

"Let's just say it makes it harder to isolate the biophysical data I look for," he said. "Insofar as I need to know what else is happening, I study that as well."

We all stood silent. I felt oddly responsible for Chase's discomfort. When I interjected, too suddenly, that I had to get going, he shot me a grateful look. To Suzanne I said, half by way of apology, "I should get those dogs from your car. They feel cheated out of their walk."

"The door's open," Suzanne said, still distracted, still curious. But she brightened. "This is all so interesting, Mr. MacMillan."

"It can be," he agreed, "when you really get into it."

I said goodbye to Suzanne and Chase outside, leaving them to some sort of fight, I sensed. She had, in fact, noticed Chase's reaction and didn't understand it any more than I did.

As I headed south along the cliffs, opting for a walk back up through the meadows instead of on the road, I ran through all the things Chase had told me about his father. Apparently he could be a real slave driver. Chase had felt it above all in school, where he'd been expected to do better than everybody else. His life in LA had been a pressure cooker of tests, private lessons, coerced community service, and competition for scholarships that would eventually fill out his college applications to places like Harvard and Yale. Nothing was ever good enough for his dad. His perfectionism as a scientist carried over into everything else, making it hard for Chase to let up even for a moment. All of this had come to a grinding halt, of course, when his mother died.

It didn't take me long on the bluffs to catch sight of another gray whale. This one rolled by itself in the surf, close enough to where the waves broke against the reefs and sea stacks offshore for me to wonder what it was doing. I felt its presence still more intensely because of the things Chase's dad had told me. Maybe his powers of concentration did close around him like a concrete bunker, and maybe he was as domineering as Chase had said. But he'd certainly struck a chord in me that day.

I watched from the bluff till the whale lifted its fluke and disappeared, sinking down to touch the bottom. I could almost see the smooth oval of calm water that formed when they did that. It was strangely poignant to me.

8

We breezed through our preseason games. We even won a tournament in Santa Rosa against bigger schools. At that point it sank in that we might be much better than we thought. We might actually have a chance to compete all the way up to the state level. Chase was the linchpin. He never scored less than twenty-five points a game and impressed everyone who saw him play, including the other coaches at that first tournament, who voted him the most valuable player.

I worried that Chase felt we weren't up to his level. He was used to much tougher competition. Once he'd let slip that some of us wouldn't even have made the team where he came from in LA. That stung a little, I admit, but he didn't say it with any malice. It was more a matter of fact. The only way I could square it bothering me was if I preferred some sort of illusion about myself, and I really didn't.

The others, though, might not have been so clear about that in their minds. It was why they could be so quick to hear the barb that Chase never gave them in things he might casually say—if only because he refrained. He kept what he thought to himself, and no one could begrudge him the right to that. Besides, we had to admit something I'd been saying all along: Chase made us better. We had more confidence on the court than we'd ever felt before. No one was quite so insecure as to scoff at the pleasure in that.

The game we all looked forward to was Fort Bragg, because we knew we had a chance to beat them for the first time in all the years of losing. There was a complicated rivalry between us that reached far back in time. Fort Bragg was the bigger and tougher town on the coast, but Mendocino had a kind of glamor on account of the picturesque beauty that brought people from all over to see it. Fort Bragg was beautiful, too, but it also had the bad luck of being a company town. The contempt of the mill owners for the people who worked for them showed in their quarantine of the town proper from the headlands, which were still fenced off and prohibited even though the various sheds and depots of the old mill stood deserted.

Mendocino lacked the same pettiness of spirit. The first settlers had the good sense to build the town up on the headlands. The logging business wasn't so industrial back then. They boomed the timber down Big River into the bay or shunted it through long sluices and guy-wire systems, milling it on the beach and hoisting it with massive cranes into the holds of the ships anchored offshore. The whole operation took place where it probably did in Fort Bragg, but people in Mendocino could still afford to live in view of the sea. They let themselves enjoy the place where they were, whether they lived in a fancy Victorian house or a shack on the beach. Everything about the layout of Fort Bragg suggested people weren't allowed to enjoy themselves.

We felt an advantage over Fort Bragg for this reason, even though, to be honest, the tensions ran just as much through Mendocino as between the two towns. The real social division on the coast was between old timers who'd been there for generations and those more recently arrived, like my mother, who'd come looking for a refuge from the outside world. These people might have blended right in like rockfish against a reef, but they brought counterculture with them, and that felt like a threat to those who'd long been there believing in hard work and a God just as inscrutable in his schemes as the mill owners on the headlands were in theirs. I suppose it was a threat. Hippies with trust funds, government transfer payments, or foods stamps behind them spelled the end of a way of life just as much as mill closures did. In fact it may have been this ending that did the hippies in as well, since what they wanted to find in Mendocino didn't exist anymore either. Nostalgia turned out to be a shared interest, spun out of the body like spider's silk or gathered like honey into beehives of the mind. It darted like a skeeter on the taut tension surface of my catch pond on Point Cabrillo, too, I admit. Those of us living on the Mendocino coast were all a little deceived about ourselves in this respect, which is why we so often missed the ground on which we did stand in common. By this I don't just mean the place where we lived. I also mean the support that place gave us when we began to see through our own illusions. This effort at self-reflection was what made real solidarity possible, even if it mostly hung in the air between us like a lost opportunity.

A few days before the big night, Chase soared in to the basket for one of those sinewy dunks and landed with one foot crooked against the wall beneath the stage, spraining his ankle. It was so severe that a doctor declared he wouldn't be able to play against Fort Bragg. As the game fell right before Christmas, Chase asked permission to start early on a trip he'd planned to LA with his father (and Suzanne, who'd never been). That meant he wouldn't even be there.

Coach blamed the high school for not tearing down that rickety piece-of-shit gym long ago. "How can anybody take themselves seriously, or expect to win games, when you have to play in a goddamn barn?" he railed in the locker room. He kicked a metal folding chair. "I wish somebody would just torch the place."

We sat there dejectedly. The news showed how much we'd come to rely on Chase. When Coach left, Fox and Zach started cursing their unlucky stars, stating flatly there was no way we'd beat Fort Bragg on our own. To our collective shame, we looked at Jordi when they said this. He'd returned once more to the starting five and settled all at once into the role of the scapegoat should we lose.

"We can't get down on ourselves," I urged, drawing attention away from this gross injustice. "We've been playing and practicing together all this time, for years now. We don't need Chase."

"They'll wipe the floor with us," predicted Fox. "Flay us fucking alive."

"Whip our skinny little asses," chimed in Zach.

"Don't say that," I cried. Their pessimism pissed me off. I thought of the advice Chase had given me in the car after that disastrous practice a month or so back. "We have to keep our cool."

To rub salt in Coach's wound, we played at home. He showed up, as he never had before, in a jacket that you could tell had hung unworn in a closet for years. It sat too loosely on his frame and reminded me of the clothes they give prisoners after their release. It was an unaccountable lapse for Coach. He never much cared how he looked to other people.

The gym was packed, as it normally would be for a Fort Bragg game. We felt more nervous than we should have while warming up. Those Fort Bragg guys we last saw at the bowling alley looked big and feisty on their end of the court. I took in the Fort Bragg cheerleaders, with Sky at the center busy shedding her heat and light on the crowd. It seemed like we were the away team.

My first good sign was seeing Ryder, for the first time ever, dole out the few dollars for a ticket and step blinking into the gym, that mitt of a bandage still on his hand. I could see how hard it was for him to come. Nervous in the best of times around other people, he looked in that crowd as spooked as he had at the hospital. His eyes wandered over the bleachers. Either he didn't see any free seats or he was having a hard time imagining himself happily wedged in next to anyone.

His solution lay up by the rafters: a small platform that once served as a perch for scorekeepers. Ryder climbed the ladder affixed to the wall and wedged himself there, dangling his long legs off the edge and propping his bony elbows on the rail. Occasionally he took draughts from a leather water bottle he wore slung across his chest, looking for all the world like a woodsman from Harlem.

His presence helped to put us in the right frame of mind. From the moment the ball was first lofted into the air at center court, and Fox out-leapt the 6'9" Fort Bragg center to tap the ball into my hands, I felt the memory of those good days at the middle school kick in for everyone. The ball went to Zach in the corner, and he nailed a three-pointer that sent the Mendocino side of the crowd into raptures. A hand turned that faucet on in his head. A minute later Coop deflected a shot by Brett Kettleman to me as I was slashing up the middle of the court. We filled the lanes. I feinted at the free throw line on the opposite end and flicked the ball to Jordi, who pulled up for a perfect bank shot from the side.

From then on the bad omens melted away. We slipped into the streamlines of Coach's system with an almost feline grace. The more we saw the Fort Bragg team hesitate, the more we hit our marks, set our picks, and ran them into the ground. We couldn't believe it. Our capacities seemed to well up and overflow. Fox felt it early in the fourth quarter, during the possession that effectively ended the game for Fort Bragg. He snagged a rebound under the basket, passed it to Zach, and took off running up the sideline, so close he practically kicked the feet of the people on the bench. He even made Coach shy out of the way, something we'd often enough been told to do in fact: flare out on the fast break, make the court bulge.

I got the ball from Zach and threaded the defense at midcourt. In the corner of my eye I saw Fox swoop in and, without thinking, lofted the ball as if he were Chase. I regretted it right away. The two of us had never practiced it before. But to our mutual astonishment, Fox took that ball at a run and rammed it through the basket as decisively as I'd ever seen him do anything. The crowd went wild as Fort Bragg called a timeout. In the adulation I glanced up at Ryder, who'd put on a pair of glasses in the meantime. At that instant he looked distinctly owlish. The contrast made me laugh out loud.

In the locker room afterward, we gave ourselves over to awed appreciation of the mystery will and effort could be when you let yourself go. We felt genuine gratitude. Coach came in grinning from ear to ear. He felt the same way, I could tell. He'd also taken off that hideous jacket.

"Helluva game, guys," he said.

"That wasn't a game," said Zach. "That was a massacre."

"They're still picking bodies off the floor!" bellowed Fox.

Coach slumped back on that same metal chair he'd kicked the other day, shaking his head. "You were savages," he observed, laughing. "You *skinned* them."

We all broke out in Indian whoops and cries, snapping towels at each other and banging on the lockers.

Later we all walked to the parking lot in high spirits. There were still numerous cars and people hanging out in little clusters. Even some Fort Bragg people were there, including Sky. She sat on the tailgate of a pickup truck talking to a few other girls. She'd changed out of her cheerleading uniform and wore a down coat with the fur-trimmed hood up. She caught my eye and waved. Then she shifted her gaze to Fox by my side.

Zach almost gasped. "Did you see that?!"

"See what?" I said. But he wasn't talking to me.

He pushed Fox into the parking lot. "Go talk to her."

Fox took off his cowboy hat and scratched his head. "Should I?" he grinned. But the adrenalin still coursing through his system was fast turning testosterone-rich, and he knew the answer.

Sky helped out by sashaying over. "Me and my friends were thinking of going to this party we heard about," she informed us. "Only we don't know where it is exactly. At some old rock star's house."

"Johnny DeLay!" barked Zach, referring to the drummer of a '70s band who'd bought one of the ranches near Comptche, the town where Fox also lived. Sometimes Johnny DeLay put on impromptu jam sessions, and those in the know enough to hear about them could show up. "It just so happens that's where we were going, right Fox?"

They didn't know where they were going, and it wasn't exactly Fox's kind of scene. Local ranchers like his dad hated Johnny DeLay. But it was as good a place as any for Fox.

"That's right," he said.

"Why don't we follow you then—if you've got a car?" suggested Sky.

"That's my truck right there," said Fox, pointing. We all looked at its chassis hiked way up over big grooved tires, the rear axle and struts defiantly exposed.

Sky ran back to her friends. Zach started asking people about rides, assuming we were all going. A caravan was arranged. I opted out on account of my mother, who was waiting for me at the Mendocino Hotel with an Irish coffee and a cigarette she shouldn't be smoking. Terry might be there, too. They'd been hanging out together more and more.

The next sign for Fox that good fortune was shining down on him was a prompt yes when he suggested to Sky that she drive with him. I smiled to see through the back window, in silhouette, Sky slide in close, the way girls do with guys like him, in trucks like that. I guessed he'd soon have his arm up on the seat back.

Fox needed reasons to let a fundamental decency in his character come out. I'd seen glimpses of it in him ever since we were kids. Back then he could be so earnestly at odds with himself. This might always be the secret of the bully, and in many respects Fox was a bully. He could intimidate and pick on people weaker than him without giving it a second thought. But he also bullied himself in people. His every impulse, thought, or decision was colored by a sense of injury so deep he only knew how to act by acting out, by doing to others what he felt had been done to him, in strange complicity with the injurer. Especially when he got drunk, or otherwise lost his inhibitions, you could see by the turbulence of his emotions just how responsible he felt for his own aggression. He suffered it like a crime he'd committed, like a guilt reaching so far back into his nature that he could no more endure it than pretend it wasn't there.

It took me a long time to figure out why he was so inwardly vexed this way. Guys like Fox, and I guess I include a lot of the people I've known who had no other reference points than that coast and its interior forests and hills, imprinted with its silences and its solitude, couldn't admit to feeling marginal. It was hardly even a choice, because admitting it took an emotional connection with themselves that they'd long ago had to break just to bear up under the weight of their own isolation. Denial served as a kind of coping mechanism. And they resented countercultural people like Johnny DeLay, who'd come looking for a version of their lives with all that weight removed or clarified, not only because such people made them feel like outsiders in their own backyards, but worse, because around them that coping mechanism no longer worked. Denial became a sign that they were marginal—a sign of having been left out of an account made elsewhere and on terms they'd never really understood. As a result they felt trapped in themselves but unable to hide, and so prey to feelings of shame that threatened a basic self-worth. Everything would have been different, I suppose, had they come to terms with their own marginality as the ground on which they did stand, and from which even the Johnny DeLays might appear more as allies than enemies. But that would have meant far more tolerance, and flexibility, than they felt they could afford and still survive. Who knows, they might have been right.

I imagine Fox got very drunk the night of the party. There wouldn't have been any other way to see the familiar landscape of his childhood change with the glamor of people who'd come from as far away as San Francisco, crossing borders more internal than anything while Zach dropped acid and turned back into the pirate he really was. There would have been a drum circle at the center of the festivities, the complexly varied beats deforming space in percussive waves that drew Fox into newly complicated depths. There would be bonfires throwing moody light into the darkness, flecked with cinders, and the smell of wood smoke reminding him of things he did know and on which he could lean for support. And he'd have fresh resources to draw on, like that game, with its proof of unsuspected talent balancing him out in his weird self-hatred.

He'd have Sky, too, in her own borderlands, following a little in his wake for what it intimated of a world beyond that Fort Bragg driveway and garage she'd told me about. Fox would see himself in the man who could help her to expand horizons. Maybe he'd also sense this manhood touching on that decency in him, on its need for expression, and wonder, in the feeling she aroused in him, if even love might be possible for a redneck like him. I hoped so, anyway.

9

The Christmas Suzanne spent in LA blew her mind. The luxurious house Chase and his dad still owned in the Pacific Palisades was set back in hills of winding streets with bougainvillea, orange trees, and views over the Santa Monica Bay. It surprised her, the splendor of Chase's other life, even if there'd always been an assurance behind his eyes and in his bearing that told you it was there.

Of course, LA proper, the long crisscrossing commercial strips and ribbons of freeway, only appeared more dismal by contrast. It was harder to feel at home there. Still, Chase showed her around to some of the cooler music clubs in Hollywood and Silver Lake, another mazy neighborhood set in the hills. In both places she had the sense that people who cared about things she did, and had similar aspirations, made lives for themselves quite handily.

Chase had contacts in the music business, friends who'd formed bands and played gigs around the city. Mostly through his mother, he also knew agents and producers. He assured her that if she was serious about pursuing a career, he could get her listened to by the "right people" when she was ready. Her answer to that was a firm decision to move to LA after we all graduated in the spring.

Back in Mendocino, she wrote songs and played music with still more abandon. Hanging out with her was like watching somebody in the middle of a wind tunnel. But the experience changed her in less positive ways, too. I noticed she stopped dressing quite so hippie-kid flamboyant: less clashing colors, hemp, or crazy hats. The long dresses dropped away. She wore tighter jeans and shoes with heels in them. Once she said to me, "I don't want to look too Mendocino all the time." I think LA made her feel a little inadequate about that.

It would have been easy enough to conclude that she'd been seduced by the glamor, but I came to find out she had her reservations as well. Something didn't seem right in Chase's life. The death of his mother hung in the air of that house in the hills like a pall, shading the opulence with a sadness all the darker because it wasn't over. If her death haunted both Chase and his father, it was in the sense of something that had happened because of feelings still very much present and alive. This had led Suzanne to think there was more to his mother's death than met the eye.

We cleared up a part of the mystery one Saturday evening. I had stopped by Chase's house around sunset with a bag of mussels I'd collected from the rocks off the Point. I thought I'd leave some for the two of them, but Suzanne persuaded me to stay for dinner. While I called my mother to let her know, Chase went to take a bath. At that point Suzanne had the idea of stealing into the studio where his dad worked—he was still away in Los Angeles.

We were both only curious about the whales at first, and went in with no other intent than to look more closely at the books on his shelves. Maybe at some level we also wanted to get a clearer idea of his research so that we could understand exactly what he did. By putting various papers, titles, and snatches of sentences together in our minds, we figured out that he also had dealings with oil companies and the Navy. His acoustic research had other engineering applications and advantages for both. Indeed, we discovered that he'd come to Mendocino to study the effects on whales of two events scheduled to take place in a month's time: a training exercise for Navy battle groups and a seismic survey to detect deposits of oil and gas off the coast. He'd even been hired to consult on and facilitate the survey with the help of a research ship that would be arriving a few weeks later.

Suzanne asked Chase about this when we were in the kitchen steaming the mussels and making a bowl of spaghetti. He confirmed that it was probably true. His father on occasion served as a consultant for corporations of various kinds.

"And you think that's all right?" she asked.

"I hadn't thought about it, to be honest. I don't really care what he does."

"He helps destroy the environment, Chase."

"Who isn't 'helping'?" he said, on the defensive now. "Come on. You use gas, don't you? You turn lights on at night, you take hot showers, you burn wood."

"No one has much of a choice about that," she said. "But your father does have a choice."

"I told you, my father's a robot. He only cares about his work. Everything else is trivial. People are math to him. They don't exist. He hurts them without even trying."

"What about the whales? Does he care about them?"

"They *interest* him, sure."

"What's the difference?"

"Interests you can calculate," Chase explained. "My father understands what can be calculated."

"He understands money, you mean."

"Okay. Money interests him, too. And those companies pay lots of money for whatever it is he gives them. He just combines the two things."

"I can't believe that."

"Why not!?" Chase cried in exasperation. "Jesus, Suzanne. I'm not denying my father's a dick, but admit it, you want what he wants: money and success."

"Not that way."

"Is there another way? Ambition comes at a price, and my father pays that price: it makes him a robot. At least he's honest about that."

"Nothing you're saying right now sounds honest to me."

"Yeah?" Chase was angry now. He wanted to silence that righteous tone he heard in her voice. "How's this: money pays for recording studios and record deals. It opens doors, it gets you fame, it gets you friends, it gets you anything you want. My father knows this. And he gets what he wants because he also knows what everything costs—every*one*, too." He spoke here from a new place of aggrieved emotion. "My mother, for instance," he said. "He knew what she cost. And believe me, it wasn't cheap."

Now Suzanne was offended. "You talk like your mother was a thing."

"She *was* a thing. A model is a thing, Suzanne. And don't kid yourself: she liked it that way. She liked the power it gave her. She had no problem with a world divided up between users and people who are used. She was the best there was at both."

"Why do I have the feeling there's something missing here?"

"Because you don't know what a world divided up that way is like." He included me in this patronizing assessment, too. "It's a world of energy and force, and it breaks you down. It's aggressive. It destroys everything around it. It destroys itself. That was my mother—a black hole of energy."

"And it killed her—"

"She killed herself," he corrected, coldly.

That ended the argument, if not the question of Chase's attitude toward the self-serving behavior that had caused him so much personal pain. It implied for Suzanne the accommodations of someone who'd had no choice but to find his emotional center around distant, soulless people, both father and mother. Indeed, as she came to see even more clearly once Chase's father returned and the two of them settled back into their daily routine in that house, the mother was the true ice queen for both. She was a deeper object of blame that surprisingly bound them together in secret sympathy. They'd formed a pact, and its terms were a common resentment of the mother for dying, for not loving them, for not being able to love anybody, even herself.

None of this excused a callous disregard for the whales, however, and Suzanne and I decided after that night, a little indignantly, to do some research of our own into underwater noise pollution. We learned that if the ocean was a vast resonating chamber for communications so subtle they made you think of sound as space, and if whales weren't so much in the water as nodes of a biological network, then the drone of ship traffic and sonar, along with many other activities like dredging for sea lanes or pipelines, altered the weft of marine life in destructive fashion. The whales felt isolated because they couldn't hear each other, moving blindly through that medium of their own sentience as if in a continuous fog. In a word, they went crazy. Narwhals stopped vocalizing for days on end. To avoid sources of acoustic trauma, minke whales swerved out of their migration routes or abandoned habitats altogether. Sperm whales broke off early from their dives or lingered longer than they should without air. Beaked whales fatally beached themselves. And those that endured the chronic disruptions, persisting in habits formed over numberless generations, gradually lost their survival instincts. They didn't know whether to stay or take flight, and so they opted for either without the sensibility they needed to understand what was actually happening.

All this confusion had consequences that affected them right down to physical tissues. The female fin whale needed to take in fifty percent more calories to birth and nurse a calf than she required on her own, and a decrease of ten percent because of changes in her life cycle slowed her birthrate by seventy-five percent. When a panicked Canary whale surfaced too suddenly, nitrogen gas bubbled in the blood, expanded massively, and blocked the passage of oxygen. A naturally deep-diving mammal died of the bends. Some scientists speculated that sonar in the water might even have activated the bubbles by itself.

One interest of Chase's dad lay in the effects of sonar on gray whales. This made it all the more disturbing that he intended to monitor and analyze those effects in the whales on their return trip up the coast from Mexico, when the oil company intended to blast air guns powerful enough to ricochet off sedimentary rock thousands of feet beneath the seabed. At the same time, the Navy training exercise would include the deployment of long-range sonar in precisely the frequencies gray whales used. It would be a one-two punch.

10

We kept winning after the New Year, with Chase back in the rotation. We did more than win. We destroyed our opponents, especially when league play started. Some of the teams we faced came from little towns that were even more remote then ours and proved hopelessly weak. It was disconcerting, to tell the truth. The fun could be undercut by the heedlessness it produced in us. I suppose I was being too fretful; I was certainly the only one who felt there was any problem. The others were too busy enjoying their power, their pride in themselves.

Fox was rushing off every night to see Sky. He showed up each morning at school lustrously satiated. Zach might have been the most improved player on the court. He'd found his stroke as a shooter and started acting on the perimeter like a real counterpart to Chase. Coop remained as solemn as ever, but there would be the occasional crack of a smile that appeared on his face. It told me winning had stirred depths in him pretty desperate for stirring, and he seemed grateful for it.

At that time I got a clearer sense of Coop's life outside school when I met his dad by chance in Boonville, a town about forty miles from the coast. We were there for a game and had time to kill while the girls' teams played, so Coop and I went into what passed for the town center—a strip of shops, inns, and restaurants—for iced coffees. He said he knew of a café that would still be open.

We found his dad sitting inside at a corner table. Coop didn't expect to find him there and, as if he felt the need to account for this, revealed that they lived near Philo, an old mill town on the road toward the coast, just on the border of the Mendocino school district.

His dad wore a bushy beard that obscured his face and fell all the way down to a big round belly. He was just as grudging in his speech as his son could be. I was taken aback to find out that he had no idea of the game we'd be playing that evening. It seemed hard to believe, not to say a little mean-spirited of him. Of course, he wouldn't have been the only parent who showed no interest in sports. My mother hardly ever came to the games either. She said it unsettled her to see me there on the court. I seemed like a grown man to her, and she wasn't quite up to the jar that could give her.

On the way back to the gym I asked Coop about his mother. He gave some non-committal answer about never having known her. "She died before I can remember."

"It's just you and your dad then?"

He nodded. I went on to talk about my mother and what it felt like having no brothers or sisters. I hoped he might warm to the topic and open up still more, but he started talking about the game instead—how we'd deal with the strengths and weaknesses of particular players, things like that. This was more volubility than usual for him, even if it did seem like just more of the usual evasiveness. But it was an improvement over simple silence.

You could hardly call people like Coop and his dad unusual in Mendocino. It attracted all sorts of anti-social types who just wanted to be alone. That was easy enough to do in those coastal ranges. No matter how long you'd lived there, it could still surprise you how big and desolate the mountains were. It surprised even me when, a week or so later, we went for another game to an inland town called Covelo. We first saw it on a curve of the highway that drops down into the flat valley where it was situated. It looked as if it had sprung right out of some 19th-century frontier. Most people who lived there were Native Americans. It bordered a reservation which included a number of California tribes that had been gathered, or forgotten, in that remote wilderness ages ago.

The game we played that night also saddened me more than any other, and made our success bittersweet in my mind. The Covelo team was particularly hapless. Everyone on it was Native American, and you could sense by their lack of training and discipline on the court just how dispirited they felt about themselves. Most were overweight, slow to react, and had trouble maintaining their stamina. It was painful to see them so at sea even in their own strategies and plays. Their coach, a white man with a kindly face who you could tell cared about his players beyond anything having to do with just basketball and winning, kept trying to keep them focused. Nothing worked.

We didn't help by slamming through them like a freight train. Coach pulled the starters soon enough, but things didn't improve for Covelo after that. Well before the game was over, they'd gotten so down on themselves that it seemed they might collapse altogether. This made Coach mad. It was like turning on the overhead lights in a bar at closing time: it ruined the drama, the moodiness, the sense of purpose. He pushed our guys to play as if the stake was his own significance, screaming at them when they messed up or missed chances, just the way he would in practice. He especially cracked the whip with Jordi, who'd returned to his ignominious role as de facto captain of the second team. I could see him on the floor feeling responsible for the need in his dad that the game not unravel. He played so hard that the whole scene began to feel a little unreal, for everyone concerned. It felt too personal, like a lid had been taken off something that would have been better left covered.

Chase was sitting next to me on the bench. The look on his face was incredulous. I could tell he was asking himself how in the world he could have come quite this far from the Pacific Palisades. At one point he leaned toward me and whispered, "Is this really happening?"

I grinned stupidly, discomfited because I understood what he meant, and it made me feel a little ashamed.

I think Coach reacted as he did because he, too, grew up in backward countryside like Covelo, and the memory of that was a source of primitive fear. His father had had a farm of 11,000 acres on the Texas-Oklahoma border when he was a boy. Half were windbreak crops for the dust storms, which were so constant no plant lasted a day without protection. Even then it wasn't easy. Season by season the farm shrank, until finally there was nothing left but uninhabitable rangeland.

Then Coach began another life of temporary work on other people's land, for other people's benefit. His family moved from town to town, digging potatoes or picking cotton. In the down times, they had practically nothing to live on. There were even stretches when they had to sleep in tents on vacant lots. The humiliation of this shiftless life burned into Coach's heart and accustomed him to fighting against circumstance with all the hatred and intelligence he had in him.

I learned these details from Terry, of course, because Coach didn't like to talk about his past. Maybe Terry had a lot to do with that. She almost died after what happened in Redding. It marked a turning point. He spent a year in a correctional facility as a result and managed to sober up. But after Terry recovered from her injuries, she found she no longer had the strength to cope with real life. Doctors had her committed to the psychiatric hospital in Napa, where she'd been a patient right up to the time she came to Mendocino.

The authorities sent Jordi to her sister in Amarillo. He stayed there for two years before Coach finally took him back. By then he'd met Anastasia, who worked as a real estate agent in Eureka, and he took a job there that had nothing to do with basketball. They got married and had two little girls, Jordi's stepsisters, and they settled down to an ordinary family life. Only after years of this did Coach start thinking he wanted to get into basketball again. He got his chance when they moved to Mendocino.

His newfound sobriety hadn't been easy to bear, but he kept his focus thanks to the memory of his past excesses and Anastasia's Christian faith. He counted on her devotion in desperate moments. Jordi, as I've said, embraced that faith still more completely, sensing the right tension needed to keep his dad from the swings of temper he remembered from childhood. It may also have been why he was always trying to convince others to believe in God. He felt we resisted at our peril.

Coach never once mentioned Terry or her appearance in Mendocino, although he obviously had to know. As far as I could tell he steered clear of her altogether. I think he feared what would happen if people found out. And it did get around. You almost couldn't help wondering why this woman wandered through town talking to herself and what it had to do with the kind of man Coach was.

Not that she stood out all that much in Mendocino. For the most part she seemed normal enough. She was quiet, but affable, and far from looking to make trouble for either Jordi or Coach. My mother didn't think she was crazy at all, but then everybody was a little half-cocked in my mother's eyes.

As far as I could tell, Terry just wanted to be closer to her son, and she never forced him to see her. She simply came to town and lived, letting proximity unweave the spells of distance and fear. The best way to coax a frightened animal from the corner it's run into is gently, with an offered hand.

You could sense the fear in Jordi, though. It made for a pressure he tried hard to contain in himself. The worst part was that he couldn't hide his efforts from the team. They were obvious in the way his downgrade to second string came to signify the complicated relationship he had with his dad. No one had to know how complicated to see that it was. We tried our best to ignore Jordi's embarrassment, but it wasn't easy, especially when we couldn't show him any particular sympathy on the court.

People tended to show allegiance by keeping their distance from Chase. While he'd become the center of the team, no one really warmed to him as a friend. This wasn't a problem for him. He had his own life on its larger scales. That put me in the awkward position of sometimes having to intercede on Chase's behalf while reassuring Jordi about where I stood with him. It may have been that he resented me a little more than the others as a result. The hint of reproach would hang silently in the air between us, making my occasional efforts at camaraderie strained and self-conscious.

One of these efforts was showing up at the middle school on occasional Sunday afternoons, where I could expect to find Jordi working on his shot after he'd come back from church. He'd be there even in the middle of the season. As unlikely as it seemed, he thought of himself going on to play basketball at the next level—a junior college if he could get on the team. His dedication was total, if also faintly desperate by this point. You could never stop thinking of how much he wanted the approval of his dad and of how grudging that approval could be.

I'd pretend to come for no other reason than boredom and rebound for him, talking around that small rift between us. But I got the feeling this wasn't working for Jordi one day when he didn't come. I waited for a good while before giving up on him, worried it might be some kind of message. I let it be my own paranoia instead.

Ryder did come, however, sprung inimitably from the ether, so the afternoon wasn't a total waste. I remarked on that bandage coming off and the marbled scar tissue on his hand, which was nicely healing. He answered by averting his gaze. He didn't want to talk about it or much of anything right then. His mind was drifty and weird. We began a mute game of HORSE that he soon lost interest in. Finally, he quit and sat down on the curb at the foot of the embankment, rolling himself a cigarette from a bag of tobacco. I sat next to him and let the silence run between us. I knew not to ask any questions, but after a while I sensed from darting glances that he might not have minded talking after all.

"Is everything okay?" I asked.

"Ohhh," he answered, drawing the vowel out as if he couldn't decide. "Not really."

"What's wrong?"

His eyes met mine, and for a moment I saw this very hurt child-like person there. "I'm wrong," he confessed.

"What do you mean?"

"In the head." He tapped his temple. "I'm not put together right." He sought a better phrase for what he was driving at. "No privacy. I can't be alone."

I had an idea of what he meant now. "You hear voices?"

He nodded.

"What do they say?"

He let me know how irrelevant this question was by ignoring it. Instead, he told me this spooky story about a "dream double" that had been planted with him in his mother's womb as part of a secret scientific experiment, and how, ever since, his thoughts had never belonged just to him. It unnerved me a little, I had to say.

"I'm misbegotten," he told me, with that vaguely biblical diction he sometimes had when he spoke. It made me wonder if he came from a tenement slum or the Harvard divinity school. "One of the mis-be-got-ten."

"You're fine, Ryder," I said, trying to reassure him. I could see something was going on in his head that he couldn't control and that it had been going on for a long time. Usually, in such a state, he would have been in one of his unreachable moods, when you knew to give him plenty of breathing room until it passed. To try for lucidity, or to ask for understanding from another, I could see him thinking, didn't make sense. But I did my best to help him through it.

As I was walking to the store for a soda later, I wondered what it would be like not being able to be alone with yourself. Mostly we fled from just the opposite. We closed ranks with other people in the fear of what we did glimpse of ourselves alone. But that, like so much else, probably had its shades of bad faith, too. Really we wanted the boundaries to be clear and firm on the inside. How exactly would they collapse when they did? By what tear in the membrane would the noise of the world enter in and undo the silence, the sense of inmost sanctuary, until there really was no escape?

As I went along thinking about this, I gradually detected the faint inflections of Jordi's voice. I paused in a pot-holed street with no sidewalks, wondering if I'd imagined it. I could have my own puzzling relations to unsourced sound. When I moved on, however, it grew all too distinct and real. I followed his voice to the saltbox house where Terry lived. Several voices burst out singing "Happy Birthday" from the backyard. I crept up the side of the house and peered over a wooden gate to see Jordi with his mother and little sisters. They were seated around a table beside a fence smothered with honeysuckle vines. Wrapped presents and a cake lay on the table.

They all had peaked paper hats on, the kind with the rubber band stretched under the chin that kids wore at parties. Together they formed an odd sentimental picture, or at least my illicit eavesdropping made it seem that way to me. I felt guilty peeking over the gate like that. I was seeing something I shouldn't. But I was slow to withdraw. I watched as they finished the song and Jordi blew out the candles on the cake—it was his birthday.

Terry took up an outsized knife she'd brought for the occasion and sliced it neatly down the middle. The two little girls clapped. She cut a large piece for Jordi, propping it against the blade of the knife and lifting both over the table. It almost didn't make it. The cake tumbled at the last moment onto his plate.

"Whoa!" she cried.

"Avalanche!" Jordi called out, pitching his fork into the white icing.

The sweetness of his smile as he did that almost broke my heart. I'd never seen him so happy, or so far away from his dad's judgment.

11

We'd broke into the top-ten ranking of best teams in California for our division by mid-season. We knew we'd be going to the playoffs well before league play ended. Our games became bona fide events, attracting more and more people curious to see just how impressive we were. Chase was the center of attention, since his play in game after game was so phenomenal. He had college scouts from big names schools all over the country sitting in the bleachers.

His first choice remained Stanford, although he held back from deciding. Coach's friend, the tall ex-teammate at the University of Oklahoma, showed up a few times to let him know there was a letter of intent to sign when he was ready. Once the man came to one of our practices. He even took a turn on the floor as a coach, helping Fox out with his moves under the basket.

Our success also rubbed off on Coach, since it came out that he might be considered for an assistant coach position at Stanford, if things continued well and he played his cards right. This raised the stakes of each game even higher. It gave a quality of almost feral intensity to the way Coach pushed us on. We all responded with genuine heart. We wanted him to have that recognition as much as we wanted it for ourselves. They were the same thing, when it came down to it.

Even Chase was surprised by his success. He knew he was good, but I don't think he'd realized just how good or how much leverage it might afford him especially with his father. If they'd made that pact together, and it united them in their common grievance against Chase's mother, it didn't stop either from resenting the other. The mood in that old lighthouse residence was one of chilly détente. This feeling was so intense sometimes that Suzanne couldn't stand to be around it. Father and son circled warily around each other, leading for all intents and purposes separate lives, with the real sources of pain going unacknowledged between them.

A basketball scholarship would mean Chase could support himself without having to rely on his father, and Suzanne, for one, saw that independence as a crucial step out of the cloud under which they both lived. But she also didn't think it was enough. If Chase wanted to change, he'd have to confront his father at those sources of pain, and that meant where they originated: in his father's coldness of heart.

It wasn't easy for her to bring this up, since it made Chase uncomfortable, and Chase uncomfortable could throw you. He grew very curt, letting you know there were boundaries that had to be respected. The difficulty Suzanne had getting past that suggested they weren't as close as it seemed. Often she wanted me around for moral support when she did try and press Chase on the subject. I wasn't sure how I felt about that, since it reminded me all the more keenly of my third-wheel status. Suzanne didn't understand this well enough for my taste, but I never mentioned it. As much of a pushover as this might have made me, I couldn't see a way of making it clear how I felt without also appearing jealous. I guess I also didn't want to rock the boat when things were going so well on other fronts. In any case, I often ended up a party to her efforts at nudging Chase toward a more honest reckoning, not only with his father but also with his own emotions.

"There's no such thing as 'neutral' love," she said during one of her attempts to sway him. The three of us had cut our fourth period classes and extended the lunch break with dessert at an ice cream shop in town. Chase shrank back into the booth where we all sat. He felt cornered.

"It's there or it's not," she said. "You care or you don't. And if you don't, it's because you've broken the connection with yourself. You've let yourself lose touch. We pay a price looking the other way, not taking stands, even on what we might think isn't important. Karma is real."

"That doesn't mean my father's going to change," Chase said. "He's going to do what he does anyway—always thinking he's right, always implying you've wasted your time on the wrong things. To his mind we should be wondering why gravity doesn't pull us all through the floor right now—that's what he cares about."

"That is kind of interesting," I observed.

"Unless you use it to intimidate people," Chase said, a little too sharply. "Believe me," he added, in a cadence of apology, "I've run up against him more times than I can count. He's stubborn. . .like the Borg."

"Don't accept that," said Suzanne.

He laughed. "Talk to my mother about it! You wouldn't believe the things she'd do just to get a rise out of him." He fell into a slipstream of recollection, sailing back into his LA world. "Once, when I was a kid, she brought home this African gray parrot that squawked all day long. She set up the cage on the porch outside the dining room where my father liked to spread his papers out on the table. She'd stand there teaching the parrot to say things like 'Go fuck yourself!' in French—'*Allez-vous faire foutre!*'—I still remember that. And my dad would just sit and ignore her, doing his work and blocking it all out. I called it Mutual Assured Destruction."

"Why did they ever get married?" Suzanne wondered.

"The same reason everybody does," Chase said. "Because we don't know fuck all about each other. We don't even want to know. We prefer our own beliefs and fantasies. We prefer what we *think* is true, not what *is* true about other people."

"That sounds a little cynical," Suzanne said.

"I'm sorry if it does," he said with a shrug. "It's been my experience anyway. My mother thought my dad was 'authentic,' unlike everybody else she knew—unlike herself, for that matter. That's why she was so wrong."

"You really hate them, don't you?"

"Is it so obvious?"

"Where does the hatred go, Chase? It has to go somewhere."

"I do tend to carry it around with me," he admitted.

"You've got to get it out."

"How?"

Suzanne drew a breath, wondering if it was worth crossing this next line. She decided to brave it. "Tell your father how you feel," she said.

⁂

I had a curious experience with Chase's father around this time. One early morning I found him sitting on the weir of the catch pond. He was as surprised as I was to see someone there and greeted me warmly, or warmly for him. He asked if I'd seen the otter.

"What otter?!"

"The river otter. It has its den over there," he said, pointing to a nearby stand of willows. The tips of their leafless branches had turned a brilliant rust-red. "I saw it from the house, believe it or not, running, or I should say sliding, in the mud next to the drainage ditch by the road. I figured it had to have its den near the pond. They like to come in and out through water."

"That surprises me," I said.

"Why?"

"I always thought I knew this place pretty well. I've been hanging out here since I was a kid. An otter's a big animal to miss."

"They can be pretty shy, even nocturnal."

"What do they eat? I don't imagine there's much fish in the pond."

"Frogs, newts. . .lots of them around here, especially in winter. There's probably fish down there, too. More than you think."

"Right."

"But I wouldn't be surprised if it ate voles and snakes as well. I'm guessing its range includes this whole headland."

"So you might see him out in the middle of the fields?"

"You'd be amazed how fast they can run."

I stood a little agape, thinking how improbable that seemed to me.

"You like learning about the natural world," he observed then.

This caught me off guard. I hadn't expected his interest.

"Yeah, I do."

"There's a mystery to it, isn't there?" he said. "Have you ever read Darwin's *Origin of Species*?"

"No."

"You should. It's surprisingly dramatic. He tells you step by step how he comes to infer natural selection from the variety of biological detail he observes. His case studies read almost like adventure stories."

"I'll look it up. Thanks."

"My pleasure," he said. "It's nice to see a young person curious about something other than himself." He meant Chase. Right away he regretted the implied criticism. "I guess that's not fair. There are different ways to be curious about the world."

This admission seemed to make him sad. I could tell his life had not been without costs. He felt a lot more than Chase gave him credit for. Of course, that only made it more puzzling why he didn't have a problem helping oil companies. That I couldn't square in my mind. I guess his good mood made me bold, because I said, hinting at these adjacent thoughts, "I like seeing how related things are. . .even things you wouldn't expect."

"Like what?"

"Otters and meadows, for instance. A doe and her fawns licking salt from beach rocks at low tide. Things like that."

"You have a feeling for systems," he said approvingly. "That's good. A biologist has to, and not only when he's thinking about space, or what they call 'horizontally,' but also 'vertically,' in time. You cut through a lot of dumb ideas when you have an evolutionary grasp of a system." He paused, searching for a clear way to explain what that meant. "For instance, people around here think that sea otters threaten abalone with extinction, and abalones are so big and abundant because there are no sea otters this far north. But the sea otter might have been precisely the reason why there are so many big abalone here, because they also preyed on the sea urchins and snails that feed on the kelp beds. This prevented the kelp from developing a toxin to protect themselves, which in turn kept the food supply abundant."

I mulled this over. "So abalone are actually declining because there's no check on the kelp feeders, which means less food?"

"There are other factors, like human predation of the sea urchins, which complicate the picture a little. But in the long run that might be exactly what's happening."

"So it would be good to get the sea otters back."

"If you can keep the abalone fishermen from killing them off."

"Right."

I saw what he meant by gaining something when you took all the different elements and causes into account—when you thought in terms of systems. But I kept coming back to why the sea otters were gone in the first place: the Russian and Portuguese fishermen who hunted them almost to extinction in the 19th Century. This raised another question in my mind.

"What happens to evolution when humans interfere in the system? Is it still the same thing Darwin said it was?"

"It's still evolution."

That confused me. There didn't seem to be any difference between what animals did and what humans did to animals. Sensing this question in my mind, Chase's dad pointed to a kite that harried the field nearby.

"Look how it keeps so low to the ground," he said. "Slow, patient, alert, shouldering into the wind, completely focused on what it's doing. Isn't that what we all aspire to: that kind of movement, that kind of mastery? Isn't it what you're trying for on the basketball court?"

"I suppose so," I said warily. Chase did sort of move confidently like that when he played. But other metaphors leapt to my mind, too: mimicry, camouflage, the arts of the preyed upon more than the predator.

"The kite is not thinking about what it's doing," Chase's dad continued, leaning on one locked arm while his free hand played accompaniment with his thought. "At least not in the way we're used to. It just goes on mindlessly regenerating itself. Again it's part of a system. A complex system, to be sure, but regular, predictable, feeding back into itself. I don't think what we admire in the kite is exactly its ruthlessness. That's too anthropomorphic. It's more in the system it traces out, with its cycles, phases, and trends, its moving equilibria, that we catch a likeness of ourselves."

"That seems kind of abstract."

"It is," he said, smiling. "I'm incorrigible that way, as Chase never stops reminding me." I saw him fight past the reproach in this to find a still deeper synthesis of his thoughts. "You might say the kite is just consciousness, feeling out its own nature, seeking coincidence with itself—except, of course, there is no bird, or body. There's only relations and differences."

He went on to talk about what happens when you engage biological systems at the level of tissues, cells, genes, and proteins. Then it really became impossible to think any other way than in terms of impersonal interactions. That was something I had next to no experience with, and it was obviously where real science took place. It had me asking if I might want to be a biologist myself one day. Could I turn my interest in the Point into a vocation the way Chase's dad did? Could I take myself that seriously?

I thought it over on the walk home a while later. At issue wasn't only my confidence, as sketchy as that might be. The science Chase's dad was talking about also involved, it seemed to me, a moral dilemma. If what oil companies, or urchin divers, or otter hunters did to a system was only a part of the system, then how did you account for its destruction except as a tendency of the system itself, a feedback loop of evolution? And if that was true, why care about preserving it, keeping it intact, "natural," the way Suzanne cared about the whales? Why be a biologist, when even the consciousness that a biologist brought to bear on life was governed by the same *self*-destructive survival instinct?

I understood, vaguely at least, that what Chase's dad meant by a system was not like, say, an electrical circuit, and that it included all sorts of variables that made it more sophisticated than a simple machine. But it was still self-referential, folded in on itself, weirdly internal, like a spider that builds a web, running back and forth across the surface it spins in the air, extruding the silk it articulates into the network of its own support. For all that the spider made a world out of nothing, the aim finally was control: reduce random forces, attract midges and flies. The spider was a vampire, I realized, and the thought stopped my heart as I went up the headland. Its intention was the drinking of blood.

Suzanne kept pressuring Chase into a showdown with his father. He shifted the irritation this made him feel onto her obsessions about whales. He could never tell her he didn't care about them in the same way she did, but he did ask why he should push a confrontation with his dad when the stakes for him weren't personal. He didn't hate his dad because of some abstract cause. He hated him unjustly, viscerally, with the finality of the door that closed on his mother in the bathtub where she died.

Despite his reservations, Chase let Suzanne bring the issue up one night at dinner on Point Cabrillo. My mother and I had been invited, too. It was the first time she'd met either Chase or his father, and I could tell she didn't like them much at all. She said nothing and sat at the table, calmly chewing her food while the conversation got heated. I think her only concern was conserving her energy enough to get back home without needing anybody's help.

As I expected, Chase's father reacted to Suzanne's questions by turning on the charm that had worked so well with me. He demonstrated how reasonably he understood the ramifications of sonar testing and the seismic surveys on the ocean environment—the "footprint" it would leave, as he put it. Then he went on to speak about how his research might help shed light on aspects of whale biology that were still poorly understood.

"There are many complex and cumulative effects that need to be sorted out," he explained, "before we can even estimate the magnitude of the problems whales face."

"It seems to me you don't need a study to tell you that ocean noise is hurting them," said Suzanne.

"But what aspects or intensities of that noise are actually causing them harm? So much is just still not clear. In some cases, we don't even understand basic biology. We don't even know for sure why whales strand themselves, for instance."

"It's because of the sonar."

"That's what we need to find out for sure."

"Why not stop using the sonar first?"

Chase rolled his eyes. He'd warned her just how easily his dad could talk people in circles. She needed a lot more than vague wishing to have any chance of convincing him of anything. As she saw this thought form in Chase's mind, he had no choice but to bring it out. "Don't be so naïve, Suzanne."

"I'd rather be naïve than sit around waiting for the gray whales to die!" she cried angrily.

"Don't sit around then," Chase's dad said. "Do something about it. But if you're serious, you're going to have to be strategic, and that's going to mean talking to lawyers, policy-makers, or military officers who will only listen to facts.

They understand cost-benefit analyses, statistics, interests. Do you think you could persuade a Navy admiral to see the issue as you do?"

"No," she groaned.

"What I'm working on right now is called a biological 'balance sheet.' It calculates the amount of energy a marine mammal spends to compensate for disruptions in its acoustic environment. It might not sound all that exciting, but at least it will make sense in board rooms and regulatory commissions."

"You're telling me that to talk to them, I have to be like them," she said. "Why would I want to do that?"

"Because you care about the whales," he replied.

She appealed silently for help from Chase. When he had nothing to offer, she turned to my mother and me. Neither of us had a ready response either. We all felt a little trapped in the way Chase's dad reasoned.

"The least you could do is not be part of the problem," Suzanne gamely persisted. "Don't take money from the Navy or the oil companies."

Chase's dad stiffened on hearing this. A sharp glance at his son told me he didn't know we'd found out about his consulting deals. He chewed in embarrassed silence, wondering how direct his next words were going to be. "Maybe I shouldn't cooperate with them as much as I do," he said slowly. "Maybe there are moral complexities that I need to take more fully into account than I have. All I'll say is there are other considerations I have to make."

"Like what?" Suzanne said.

"*Personal* considerations, if you must know." He cast around for an example that wasn't too personal. He opted, at last, for a paternal grab at Chase's shoulder. "Like putting this guy through college."

Chase instantly disliked the gesture. "Don't involve me in this," he said, shrinking away. Now it was his dad's turn to feel trapped.

"I meant a father has responsibilities, that's all." He turned to my mother. "It's not easy being a single parent, is it, Cadie?"

The sudden attention made her nervous, but her standard wit did not desert her. "I'm a dog before her bone," she said with her mouth full of food, both arms flanking the plate on which she fixed her ironic gaze. "My motto is: don't come between a father and a son. You never know who's going to get hurt."

"Mostly it's the son," said Chase.

His father glared at him. It was a low blow. Coldly he said, "You know as well as I do that some things around here have not been negotiable."

I had the feeling he was thinking of his wife, and particularly of the pressure she'd put on them both to live up to social standards that might not have come naturally to him at all. They may have for Chase, though, and this suggested still another layer of the disaffection between them. I imagined all three standing on a platform, balanced in empty space on a single fulcrum, tilting this way and that. On it alliances were made and broken, with two always ganging up on one.

"Maybe you don't need the Navy or oil companies the way you think you do," Suzanne offered, when it became clear Chase wasn't going to speak.

His father leaned back in his chair. "They're going to do what they do anyway," he declared. "I can't stop them. I'm not even sure they *should* stop. The truth is we need them to be out there, for lots of reasons, whether we like to admit that or not." He spoke without conviction now, like a man weary of his own arguments. He also quite distinctly linked this back to his troubles with his son when he said, "We live in a very complicated world, I'm afraid. . ."

But Suzanne had stopped listening. The echo, in his first remark, of what Chase had earlier said about him—that he did what he did anyway—reverberated through her mind like a thunderclap. In its expanding waves of shock she knew all at once what she would do: organize resistance in town against the use of sonar off our shores.

She threw herself into the task, talking to people, putting up flyers, organizing meetings. I saw it strain her relationship with Chase, who found himself awkwardly in between her and his father. Not that there turned out to be more opportunities for the topic to come up. Shortly after that dinner the research vessel put in at Noyo Harbor, and his dad spent most of his time from then on preparing for his fieldwork.

I saw the ship a few days later, swaying in the swell off Point Cabrillo. Its deck was crowded with winches, cranes, windlasses, and other gear. The sun bounced blankly off the bridge windows and rimmed the white stanchions. It looked as reasonable and reassuring as Chase's dad.

I had the idea of introducing Suzanne to Zach's parents. They knew a lot of people in Mendocino with experience as political activists—old-timers from the '70s and others still working against everything from climate change to toxic waste at the local dump. They told me they also might have some contacts for her in groups like Earth First! in the Bay Area.

One day I took her and Chase up to where they lived on Navarro Ridge. The place was dispiriting to visit: the yard full of junk and the house a hopeless clutter. This was mostly because Zach was the only robust caretaker, and he didn't have much discipline, as you might imagine. All three of them had a packrat mentality.

Suzanne and Chase were taken by surprise when they saw Zach's parents for the first time. Chase had no idea what to make of them laid up in bed in their living room. It must have been another one of those moments when he felt far away from his LA world. He looked uncomfortable, and that was too bad, because Zach resented him for it. Zach was very protective of his parents, and it pissed him off any time he felt they were being blamed for their infirmities.

We learned a lot about political activism that day. We heard a few of his parents' adventures, which included cat-and-mouse tactics against logging crews at the Enchanted Meadow up in Humboldt, car chases, sabotage, and police treachery. They also gave us more mundane advice about call-in campaigns, petitions, tabling, telephone trees, and so on. It turned out there was a lot of technique to protest, a fact Suzanne appreciated as a musician. They went together in her mind.

Driving back to town in her Datsun 510 afterward, she reproached Chase for his aloofness in front of them. "What can I say?" he said coolly. "They gave me the creeps."

That made me mad, but I kept quiet in the back seat. I let Suzanne do the fighting for me.

"You're so judgmental, you know that?" she said.

"I'm being honest, that's all. I don't mind them being the way they are. It's just not the way I am."

"It's more than that," she said. "It's personal, I feel it. You don't like them. . .or people like them. They're too close to something you don't want to be close to."

"All right," he conceded. "They seem a little defeated to me. And I don't feel that way. I don't want to feel that way. Who would?"

"That's not it," she went on, shaking her head. "You don't like them because they took a stand and now they're paying for it. They show what it costs to fight the system."

"Now who's judging?"

"You're not really interested in fighting the system, are you?"

"I don't know what you mean by 'the system.'"

"You like the world the way it is, no matter how much you complain about it."

"I *take* the world as it is," he said. "I don't pretend it's something else."

"What do you stand for, Chase?" she asked angrily now. "I mean, really? What do you care about enough to risk your life for it?"

"Nothing I can't touch anyway."

"What crap," she retorted. "You mean nothing that's not good for Chase MacMillan."

"Fuck you, too," he said.

12

We played the last game of the regular season once more against Fort Bragg, this time in their gym. We'd already won the league title and were looking forward to home court advantage in the upcoming playoffs. Coach, however, wouldn't let us take them for granted just because Chase was with us this time. It turned out he had nothing to worry about. We beat them even more soundly.

The trouble came after the game, when we all emerged from the locker room and headed for the bus. Zach could think about nothing but his eighteen points, a high for him. "I was smoking," he said. "I couldn't miss. Next time I get that feeling I'll tell you, just so you know you've got a miracle on your hands and his name is Zach fucking Mayerson!"

"You're the man," said Fox, forgetting everything the next instant when he caught sight of Sky. He didn't so much walk as swoon forward to meet her. She threw herself on him, planting one hard provocative kiss on his lips. It held us all a little too long in its spell. When she let go, her eyes went straight to Chase, who was standing next to me. I saw the shift of interest in her gaze make the previous display of affection a little insincere. Chase felt it, too. There was immediate electricity there, and all I could think to do in my alarm was hurry us on to the bus.

"Have we met?" she asked him.

"I don't think so," he said.

Fox stood icily by. So did Zach, for that matter. The next moment Sky defused the tension by slipping her arm in Fox's and leaning a coy forehead against his shoulder. Everybody understood by that where the lines were drawn. Chase himself moved on without even telling her his name. I followed after him, relieved. As I've said before, you could count on Chase to know things in dimensions that weren't obvious. But I also couldn't help thinking how Sky's luxuriant blond hair, blue eyes, and frank sexual presence resembled my image of his mother.

I guess I've established by now that it was my temperament growing up to be a watcher. I stood off to the side and noticed things, looking to the larger patterns in which they fit. In a lot of ways it wasn't much fun. I sometimes felt like a civil trespasser in other people's lives while my life moved on its relatively anonymous course without too much variation. I was good old Woody, the friend everybody could trust and take for granted.

In many respects I found it a comfortable role to play, but it wasn't without risk. I worried that my cool temperament was slowly settling me into too much heaviness of spirit—until, finally, all I'd be was spirit, with no perspective or even will of my own. That was the problem with my kind of sensitivity: it drains decision out of you with perfect subtlety. What remains is a pure receptive surface that records everything except the recorder.

At some point I would have to be more honest about this risk. It was one thing to know, as I think I did, that I was a part of the world I observed. It was another to really feel it. To the extent that this knowledge was still abstract to me, I might have thought I could stay outside or above things, protected against life's shocks in my desire to understand what was happening around me. What I didn't understand, though, was that this self-deception still involved me in the world. It made me a little like Chase's dad, for instance, when he looked the other way or hid in his science. It made for less sensitivity than I imagined, even as I imagined I *was* being sensitive.

Something would have to give here. I couldn't remain a spectator of my own life this way forever. It turned out I wouldn't have long to wait. My day came on the headlands of Point Cabrillo when, a week after that last game, I saw Chase with Sky on the bluffs.

She may not have met him before that second Fort Bragg game, but she'd seen him in Noyo Harbor when the research vessel had attracted the attention of everyone who worked down there, including her older brother. On a day he spent readying his boat for a week out crab fishing, she'd come by with some provisions and noticed Chase drop his father off in the BMW.

I haven't stressed enough how handsome Chase was. He could cause a stir unlike anything I'd seen simply by entering a room. In fact, I remember him saying that his mother was the kind of woman who "dominated a room." This power of attraction he inherited from her was double-edged. It made people feel their own inadequacies as it also prompted in them longings for richer experience.

Chase understood this effect he had on others very well; he counted on it as much as he let you feel his indifference to it. He might have had to, since people were quick to condemn any sign of calculation in him. It was one of his more impressive achievements that he never left this judgment much room for good faith. That isn't to say he lacked in calculation. He knew how to play his hand, that's all.

Sky recognized him during the game, where, of course, his brilliance was on full display. She must have resolved then to meet him, and it turned out to be a simple matter of asking about the ship in Noyo Harbor until she found someone willing to give her a phone number. I gathered when she called him out of the blue one night that she made it clear how she felt. The game she played at this other level was new to her, and she started with what she had to offer. It must have worked.

There was almost two weeks before the first playoff game. We had daily practices right up to the end, but Coach gave us the last day off with orders to rest up. I was on yet another of my dog walks when I caught sight of Chase and Sky strolling at the cliff's edge, not far from the lighthouse. They were waiting for the sun to go down. Both wore heavy wool sweaters and seemed from my vantage point at ease with each other, like figures out of the New England clothing catalogs my mother sometimes received in the mail, denizens of tony rowing clubs and yacht harbors. All of a sudden Point Cabrillo had become Martha's Vineyard.

The discovery of their relationship threw me into confused meditation on questions of trust and betrayal. I couldn't understand by what turn of the heart people became capable of cheating on others. This absence of guile in me raised another question, too: the relation it implied to my underlying caution, to what held me back from my own desires. Maybe love was always a matter of guile, of deceit even. Maybe it was a game people played with as much cunning as they could, and I was fooling myself if I believed I could love, or be loved, without also playing the game.

I said Chase was handsome. People almost couldn't help commenting on it. But he could also be careless when his needs clashed with those of others. I saw, finally, that he had little sense of responsibility and even less respect. Was he handsome because he was careless? Was it his indifference that we found admirable, his self-love that we found seductive and daring?

I might have reproached Suzanne right then for liking Chase at all, or for not seeing how I was different from him in this regard. But could I really blame her? I'd been admiring Chase all along, too. I felt his allure as much as anyone. It pulled me toward Sky and Chase on those bluffs with a fascination whose price I could precisely measure by the distance between us, the flat field of wet grasses, the wind sheeting the sea beyond, the lighthouse in its serene immobility on the Point ceaselessly revolving its signature flash through the oncoming night. My very presence there may have been bound up with confused aspirations for love and exception that Chase had only further aroused in me.

There were even more anxious dilemmas to sort out. Suzanne and Fox were my friends. What was I supposed to do: keep what I'd just seen to myself because it was none of my business and spare them the hurt they'd feel, or tell them because it was their business and I cared for them, far more than I cared for Chase or Sky. But if I told Suzanne, would it be out of care or envy? And if I told Fox, would he hate Chase so much he couldn't keep playing on the same team with him? How should I weigh the respect I owed to him with that I owed to everyone else? Was winning more basketball games worth the lie I would have to maintain, or was lying just another kind of respect?

Confounded by these questions, I couldn't bring myself to make the walk back up the headland. Instead, I sat close by the catch pond as night closed around me, listening to the frogs, thousands of them, float their noisy satisfaction to the stars. I did manage to remind myself that I couldn't say for sure just what I'd seen, or if it weren't, in fact, more innocent than I thought. I had to know more definitely what was going on before I could decide what to do.

With the suppression of scruple that comes, I suppose, with any action you can't credit in yourself, I tied the dogs to a fence post and crept through the darkness toward Chase's house. I fought myself all the way around the compound of residences, where I entered the yard from the pitch-black cover of the cypress trees that stood in back. No lights were on in the house, but I detected the flicker of a fire in the window that opened onto the living room. I shuffled against the siding and peered through a pane. I saw Chase reclining on a sofa. Sky, with her back to me, sat beside him on the floor. Her long blond hair glimmered in the firelight. Both were naked. She was sucking his cock.

But far worse than anything they might have been doing, I saw Chase looking straight back at me. In his eyes was the knowledge, as clear as his shock and my shame, that whatever I was doing there, it meant I wanted *him* with a passion that was far out of proportion to the friendship we had. I'd been found out. . .in all sorts of ways.

That knowledge in Chase's eyes followed me up through the fields, which I chose over the road even though I could barely see the path. My humiliation was so intense that I winced at imaginary blows as I went. The night had turned into something else altogether.

I put off returning home. My mother would see I was upset, and I didn't feel up to fending off her questions. Once I'd reached the lawn beside the trailer park, I sat on a picnic table and waited for the adrenalin to run its course. I had this irresistible urge to writhe and twist, like an epileptic in seizure. I thought about doing it right there. . .acting it out. Nobody could see me, so what did it matter? Instead, I wrapped my knees tightly in my arms and tensed up, watching the lighthouse beam wheel through the night.

I must have lost track of time this way, because the dogs, who'd been sitting quietly by the table, aware that something was wrong, eventually lost patience and wandered off. I only found out when I saw a flashlight catch the dew in the grass and heard a person approaching from behind. It was Miriam. She had the dogs on their leashes.

She waved hello. I nodded sideways from under my hat, trying to conceal my agitation, which only betrayed it more, even in the dark. She stood by, wondering if she should let me be. After a while, however, she decided to join me on that picnic table and stare out over the headland. She thought she might be able to see what I saw. When that didn't work, she took out her pad of paper and wrote in the light from her flashlight: *Are you okay?*

I shook my head.

What's wrong?

I remembered what Ryder had said when I asked him the same question. I replied in my crude sign language: *I'm wrong.*

Miriam rolled her eyes.

You seem pretty right to me, mister.

Her sympathy put me at ease enough to consider telling her what had happened. I could get all my remorse out in one penitential confession. But I'd have to write it down and that was far too daunting a task right then. I wouldn't even know where to begin.

You want to come inside?

She gestured back toward her trailer, where lights shone in the windows. I thought about her husband Daniel. I definitely didn't want to see him.

He's not home. He won't be back till tomorrow.

She mistook my reluctance for temptation. I took the pen from her. She sat to my left, so I had to lean in close to write on the pad, which she kept on her lap.

I'm pretty confused right now.

She wrote her response. *There's a lot of that going around.*

I sensed a sadness in this admission, the weight of a life long since given over to resignation. Miriam suffered without complaint, but she also suffered more than you knew.

I wrote, *I feel like I'm drowning in three inches of water.*

Miriam's right arm went around my waist as I leaned in and she read. I sensed her hand push reassuringly into my coat and squeeze, then retract back again into the space between us.

That doesn't mean the feeling isn't real.

I cocked my head quizzically. She tried to explain.

It's one thing to say you're feeling sorry for yourself. It's another to deny your feelings have any worth.

That cut delicately to the bone. *Do you always know the difference?* I wrote.

Sometimes we need other people to help us out.

How do they do that?

She paused, mulling over an answer. Then she wrote: *They draw us out of our private worlds. They seal our unreal feelings with a touch.*

I stared into the darkness, her gentle lyricism stirring the ache in me all over again. This must have aroused in her more tenderness than I realized, because a moment later she reached up to remove my hat, laid it on the table, and began running her fingers softly through my hair. This intimacy came as a shock. It had an element of passion in it that I wasn't ready for at all. I'd never once thought of Miriam in that way. I was still a kid around her. Changing that idea of myself, however slightly, made me feel a little violated, if not also, in a manner still more perplexing, violent in my aversion. I concluded from this that violation was general in the world and the only response that made any sense was the instinctive one of flight.

I stood up on the bench, jumping to the grass. "I–I have to go," I said, even though I knew she couldn't read my lips.

I called the dogs, grabbing at their leashes. She looked crestfallen but also guessed at independent motives in my sudden panic. She scribbled onto her notepad, which I hardly had the wherewithal to read when she thrust it at me. It said:

Shyness can be mean. Love yourself, Woody.

I nodded idiotically, pulling the dogs after me and heading off toward home as if I was one step ahead of catastrophe. I even left my hat behind.

As if I didn't have enough to deal with that night, my mother suffered another bad fit of coughing. I had to put all my dumb agony aside and help to calm her down. She rarely cried, so when she did it unnerved me. It indicated the extent of her fear. She kept saying through her tears that she was cold, freezing cold, and no amount of blankets I threw over her seemed to work. I started a fire in the cook stove and drew her as scalding hot a bath as our water heater would bear. When I told her the bath was ready and threw back the covers, she lay there in an asthmatic stupor.

"I can't get up," she said.

"Yes, you can. I'll help you." I slipped my hand behind her back, raised her from the pillow, and swung her legs over the edge of the bed. She had all her clothes on, even her boots. I grabbed her inhaler and placed it over her mouth. Her hand drifted up. I helped her to pump it the first time, but she managed herself after that, breathing in her meds as best she could. Then she sat shivering.

Carefully, I lifted her to her feet. She swayed into the old stiffness of her once broken hip and froze. "Lean on me," I urged, and we walked through the door to the bathroom together, where I sat her on the toilet. I could tell she wouldn't be able to undress on her own, so I unlaced the boots and pulled them off. After that I slipped the two pairs of wool socks down around her heels. I hesitated a moment. I'd never had to do this for her before.

"I'll unbutton your shirt," I said. She averted her face and pressed her lips and eyes shut, nodding again. It was awkward for both of us. I slowly undid each button, revealing the pale skin beneath, her full breasts swimming in her bra, her belly a little rounder than I remembered it. She'd lost a lot of her normal muscle tone only lately. This brought the tears brimming into my eyes.

"I'm sorry, Woody."

"There's nothing to be sorry for." I raised one arm, then the other, peeling the shirt off. I undid her belt and unbuttoned her jeans, pulling them from off her hips and legs. She reached around for the hooks on her bra, trying her best to rally for my sake, but I just undid them and took it from around her shoulders. Her breasts sagged to her belly, drawing her, it seemed, into a forward hunch.

"I'll get you into the tub," I said.

Lifting my mother was no easy feat. She wasn't tall, or even that big, but she had heavy bones and an iron constitution. I took a deep breath, bracing one arm under her knees and the other around her back, and lifted her altogether off the toilet. I could smell the sebum in her hair as her head fell against my cheek, the ammonia of her flesh as her shoulder pressed against my body. Never more than in that moment did I feel just how dependent she was on me and how much strength would be required of us both in the future. It turned everything upside down in my already roiled heart: mothers and sons, men and women, love and hate.

I took her to the hospital in Fort Bragg. The doctor said she had no choice but to start using an oxygen tank. I told her that she would quit smoking as soon as the season ended, even if it meant I had to keep her on a leash. She reluctantly agreed.

I was exhausted that night. The home game seemed to pass in a dream. I couldn't gauge the right distances of bodies, hands, lines on the court, digitized numbers on scoreboards. I dribbled and wondered if the ball would come up again. And I was the center, the locus, of the team. If I missed a read, the whole composition could unravel. Coach screamed at me from the sideline, confounded by my lapses.

The game stayed tight until the very end. Only Chase's ability to take over kept us from losing for the first time. Well before then Coach had put Zach at the point and sent Jordi in for me. I sat at the end of the bench, trying to get that bead in my head back to level. As I said, we're all the way in the world whether we like it or not. There is no getting around this, and no fairness either. I suppose that's why I didn't end up saying anything about Chase and Sky.

13

I managed to recover my wits on the court. I pushed past my pain and returned to my reliable self. We won two more games to earn a shot at the regional championship in Ukiah. If we won there, we'd go to Sacramento for the state tournament, which would be hosted in the arena where the Kings played. That, as Zach liked to put it, was the big time. We talked about it constantly, filling the prospect out in our excited imaginations, even though we first had to beat the best team we'd yet faced. They were also undefeated and ranked higher than we were. One of their players had already signed a letter of intent to a Division 1 school.

We had a reputation by then as a disciplined team that played well together. We also weren't without talent. Chase, of course, was a phenomenon. He attracted interest all over the country. But some of that interest had rubbed off on Fox, too. A number of schools had begun paying attention to him. More than any of us, Fox had the athletic ability to play at the college level. This prospect made him think hard about it for the first time. It offered a way out of that ranch in Comptche, if he really wanted it. I think he did, even though he still had trouble believing anything would be good for him in the wide world. He was his own worst enemy. For this reason more than any other, I hoped he wouldn't find out about Sky.

Chase and I talked about it only one time. He didn't particularly want to discuss it even then. It pissed him off that he would have to justify himself to me.

"What's the big deal?" he said. "I fucked Sky. You would've, too, if she'd thrown herself at you the way she has me."

I stated the obvious. "What about Suzanne?"

"She has her own distractions, doesn't she? If she didn't, this whole thing might not have happened." He heard the lie in that right away. "Or it might have," he said. "I don't know. I'm not sure what's going on between us right now."

"What about Fox?"

"He doesn't need to find out, unless Sky decides he does. The same goes for Suzanne. As far as they're concerned, it hasn't happened. In fact," he added, as a new variation on this theme occurred to him, "it *hasn't* happened."

The shift of emphasis hung between us. "That seems cold," I said.

"Maybe so," he said curtly. "I would've thought it was common sense."

"It's not for me."

"Oh, fuck!" he cried, letting his irritation get the better of him. "I'm so tired of this fake idealism, in you and Suzanne both. It's so lame. And it's not honest. You know it's not, or you wouldn't be spying on me at night. You'd have your own stupid life to worry about."

I couldn't say anything to that. I'd lost all credibility in his eyes. And my recognizing this only angered him more.

"That's the difference between us, Woody," he said then, unable to help himself. "You're outside the window looking in, and I'm the one you look at. I have a life, and you don't."

That went through me like a bullet. I suppose the fact that it hurt so much meant I agreed with Chase. I wanted his approval enough to care about his judgment. Indeed, I reproached myself for this, and the reproach became still another intensification of the pain, another way of feeling like the loser he saw in me. It seemed so circular, and so inescapable. I was in the world all right, only it was Chase's world. A world where opportunism was a virtue and looking out for yourself was the only right thing to do. If you hesitated, you were missing the point of the game being played. If you objected, you were an "idealist." Your perceptions had no value, no weight, no reality. They existed as I did outside that window—in the dark and in the cold. And when you really felt that, invisibility became a way of life.

The snag, if there was one, Chase felt in the hidden costs of this worldly calculus. They carried over in the equations as a remainder: an absence of love so intense it broke the very instinct for survival. We were supposed to have endless reserves for the play of forces that calculus described. We were supposed to bounce back in its field like cork on the sea. Nothing should hurt. His mother's death thus complicated everything, and the problem it posed for him wasn't just how to mourn her loss but how to re-establish the balance she'd upset by managing to hurt him.

I think Chase struggled with both sides of this problem. He'd been smart enough to glimpse a chance at feelings different from what he'd known in LA, but it meant giving something up. It meant finding a common ground in the hurt he saw in me. It meant seeing *himself* in the loser we all are as human beings, wanting grace and missing it, too. When Chase couldn't do this, he drew back into what he knew, re-establishing his balance, keeping his cool. Everything became subtle once again, but he had claimed his immunity. Fucking Sky made perfect sense at that point.

Yet he knew it didn't. I liked to think that he could feel his self-possession sealing him off a little more tightly with each small failure to find that common ground. The distance that had set in between him and Suzanne gave him its proper measure. Before he started entertaining Sky on the Point, Suzanne had already begun withdrawing from the world in which his glamour had gotten its true colors. She might not have known why she did it, and she might have suffered temptations to compromise for the sake of recognition or fame, but she would slip the knot as easily as Chase tied it in the end. He knew this, too. He may even have wanted to get back at her for it.

For the past several weeks she'd been devoting herself to organizing a demonstration against the seismic survey. The issue caught on with a lot of people because it implied the next step of revoking the moratorium on oil drilling. This would have turned many on the coast into ecoterrorists overnight. The outrage grew when Suzanne discovered that neither the Navy nor the oil company had bothered to obtain authorization under provisions of the Marine Mammal Pro-tection Act. The government had more or less been looking the other way as a matter of course; compliance with the regulations had been lax to non-existent for years.

Suzanne made sure of a public outcry this time. The news raised the stakes of the demonstration, as it might actually mean they could stop the survey cold. The Navy had already commenced its exercise on the outer continental shelf. In what I considered a stroke of brilliance, Suzanne decided to hold the event on Point Cabrillo, right in front of Chase's dad and in view of the gray whales. They'd started appearing on the route back to their Bering Strait feeding grounds.

I helped her out by building a makeshift stage next to the lighthouse. I had a lot of fun soaking up the bustle of preparation on the Saturday afternoon before the event. It gave me a fresh perspective on the headland, sawing wood and banging nails while swallows cut the air, kites hunted in the fields, and ospreys high overhead relayed back and forth between sea dives and nest. The place I knew better than anywhere else had changed for me in previous weeks, maybe irrevocably. But on that day I sensed none of it might have mattered in the ways it seemed. I might even have wanted the changes.

Of course, the next day turned out blustery and cold, with what looked suspiciously like a storm cell on the horizon. Suzanne learned right before the demonstration that the National Marine Fisheries Service had given the okay to the oil company at the last minute. This became the first announcement from my stage. Things don't ever work out quite the way you hope they will. Still, at least two hundred people showed up to hear speeches by the activists, lawyers, and environmental specialists that Suzanne had arranged to come. They included all types, from bedraggled old hippies living on disability checks to solemn fishermen who had their own interests at stake. I saw Daniel, Miriam's dour husband, among them.

People with other agendas also worked the crowd. I noticed some earnestly passing out leaflets with the photograph of a seven-year-old boy abducted from a street in Ukiah two days before, along with a rough pencil sketch of the man who'd last been seen with him: middle-aged, shaggy hair, beard, not much more distinctive than that. They managed to persuade a news crew that had come all the way from San Francisco to include a plea for information in their live report. Collaborations like this made the day more communal and festive than I had much experience with outside of school. We even had a visit from a few gray whales, their glistening backs just visible in the rough sea.

The demonstration ended with Suzanne singing some of her songs with a backup band. She'd invited me to accompany her on the mandolin. This time I overcame my shyness enough to join in. I couldn't play worth a damn, as I've said, and I missed notes more often than not trying to keep up with her band. But it didn't matter. It's almost impossible to make a mandolin sound bad. All I had to do was listen to the chord changes and play the rhythm as best I could for it to add tone to Suzanne's bell-like voice.

From the stage I could see Chase in the crowd, huddled in a down ski jacket. He'd been around the whole day, showing what I thought was token support. He looked uncomfortable towering over the people around him, with the vague expression on his face of the near-sighted trying to focus distance. He had more going for him than anybody there, than anybody I'd ever known. He could probably still have Suzanne if he had enough sense to recognize a good thing when it was right in front of his eyes. But just at that moment I wouldn't have wanted to trade places with him.

§

Chase's dad had in fact already left on his research vessel to monitor the commencement of the Navy exercise, which involved some thirty ships and submarines about twenty miles off the coast in one of its specialized acoustic training areas, or "complexes." The simulation of combat and surveillance tactics included detonations of high explosives and ordnance firing, as well as the use of various sonar systems mounted on hulls, air-deployed from helicopters and fixed-wing aircraft, or dropped as floating sensors. Waves of sound accordingly swept the ocean, bouncing off the sea floor and striking not only enemy ships but everything that moved in it.

The diffraction patterns could be dazzling in their complexity. They looked like visualizers on the computer screens that Chase's dad used to model the variations of signal he was interested in, too slight for the untrained eye to detect. He looked in particular for the effects of the new sonar system that was being field-tested for the first time. They called it ROMEO-78. It consisted of numerous transmitters fixed to a cable and lowered into the water through a slot in the hull of an old pipe ship the Navy had adapted to this use. Designed for the vastness of the open sea, it emitted signals powerful enough to reverberate across the entire North Pacific Basin. It demonstrated a range many orders of magnitude higher than any previously existing system. The impacts on marine life could be severe: internal hemorrhaging, rupture of organs, embolism, permanent hearing loss, and suppression of the immune system. It would cause unprecedented confusion for the whales: a ringing in the inner ear that forced them to extreme adjustments in the vicinity of the frequency, with a corresponding loss of vital information—the call of a calf or a potential mate, an approaching killer whale. Nonetheless, as Chase's dad had told us, the incoming sonar data would help biologists to move beyond conjecture where the energetic limits of baleen whale hearing were concerned.

14

I think of the game in Ukiah like one of those "Victory at Sea" warships in the middle of a storm, lifted onto cresting waves and dropped down sheer walls of water into long troughs. The gym, for all its immobility, seemed to float on its foundations. Those who came to watch us had noisily packed it out like lashing rain or sea spume. The only link to the world outside was a regular ping of placeless sonar.

The other team played a fast game. Coach had said that would be to our advantage, since it meant whatever happened, we'd win on our strengths. All we had to do was outrun them. But from the start it appeared they might have more stamina. We'd been trading baskets the way boxers would punches through the first half. Still, we fell behind.

Everyone was on except Cooper. Chase hit his jumpers and Fox his little hook shots under the basket. Zach and I had the press cooking at midcourt. But Coop couldn't find the usual rhythm of his game. He had the same severe tension in his jaw and the same blank determination in his eyes as he always did. If anything, he seemed even more implacable. Despite all that, he moved around the floor like a man in a maze.

At halftime Coach came in to the locker room livid. He got right up in Coop's face, pulling him off the bench and pinning him against the locker. His eyes were hard, glittery. He dominated with his squared shoulders and cocked hip.

You saw in such moments that Coach was a man who knew how to fight.

"No one is going to lose this game!" he shouted. Coop turned away from him without looking anybody in the eye. He wouldn't let himself be read. "You go out there and play the way I know you can." Coach spoke to everybody now. "You make this game *swing*, understand? You give every ounce you have to closing that gap." He glared again at Coop. "And if you don't, I'll kick your goddamn ass!"

The third quarter picked up where we'd left off. We played some of our best basketball, but the other team moved just a little farther ahead. We could do nothing more than feel the engine give in its failing cylinder. At one point we thought we'd cut the lead to seven after Zach stole a pass and winged it to Chase for a long three-pointer. But as the ball arced to the basket, Coop slammed so hard into another player that a technical foul was called. The shot didn't count.

The crowd booed. It was pretty flagrant. Coop stood dazedly in the midst of the derision while a referee reported the call to the scorekeepers. I came up to reassure him. I thought the problem had only to do with the effort to come back and recover his presence on the court, but when I placed my hand on his shoulder, I felt all at once that the loneliness in him was far more serious than any of us had thought. It went beyond any possible significance of the game.

In fact he didn't care about the game at all. I saw his eyes shift as though seeking some place of escape. And then, to my horror, he ran out from under my touch and rammed his head into the nearest wall. He wobbled to the floor and passed out.

Cooper had to be carried away on a stretcher. Everyone milled around the court, too stunned to speak. They assumed he'd snapped under the pressure, but I found myself thinking back through the years of enigma in him to what might have been a silent plea for help all along. He gave you so little to hold on to. He offered nothing and expected nothing, and we'd almost had no other choice but to respect his privacy. Now I wondered if we hadn't just been careless.

The game resumed in deadly earnest. Jordi, taking over at the forward position, swarmed around guys half a foot taller than him. His desperation added a further dimension to the shock we felt at Cooper's breakdown. It held us in terror at the prospect of the whole season ending right there. We couldn't believe it. Somehow it wasn't supposed to happen this way. It hadn't come to its proper term in our minds. We felt like we were supposed to win, like we'd already won. It turned out to be more than wishful thinking. As the game wound down we slowly made that lead mercurial.

The swing came at the very end. Fox made two quick baskets. Zach pulled off a spectacular save that had him tumbling ass over head into the other team's bench. Jordi reached around the Division 1 recruit and slapped the ball into the forecourt, where I scooped it to Chase on the run. I watched as he threaded two defenders, leapt from near the free throw line, and threw down a dunk that set the whole gym roaring. We trailed by one point with ten seconds to go.

Coach called a timeout. We huddled together on the sidelines. He was angry with us for not slowing down to set up a last three-point shot, but the spirit of his game was nothing if not reckless, and we had the momentum now. That couldn't be denied.

The roar hardly wavered through the two minutes and intensified still more as we moved back onto the court. The referee handed the ball to one of the other team's players under the basket. Fox harried the inbounds pass. It bounced to my man, their point guard, who'd been a half step ahead of me probably the whole game. I reached in to foul him, thinking I'd just screwed up.

But then dumb luck showed its crazy hand. As I reached in, the guard dribbled up the sideline and the ball slipped free of his control. It rattled around like a hockey puck in his legs. I cut right through his stride as the ball bobbled into my possession. Before I knew it, he'd fouled me. The whistle blew, and we both looked up. Five seconds remained on the clock and I had a one-plus-one free throw coming.

Now the crowd's roar reached such a pitch that it almost ceased to be noise. It seemed to open this paradoxical space of silence and stillness on the court, into which I could slip like a kid under blankets. Nothing could touch me there. The other coach sensed this, too, I could tell because he made me wait through two long timeouts. At one point Coach seized me by the shoulders and gazed straight into my eyes, looking for nerve enough to stay right where I was. He seemed to see what I felt, that invisible space. It reassured him. He flashed me a toothy grin.

Finally, they let me walk to the free throw line and wait as the other players took up their positions around the key. Fox and Zach pumped their fists. Chase tugged the bottom of my jersey. Jordi concentrated with all his might on the rebound should I miss the first time. I felt his most complicated hopes in the way he leaned, straining into the key.

I hefted the ball in my fingers, bent my wrists down to get the feeling of that circle Coach had told us about, and focused on the front end of the hoop. The roar of the crowd was perfect. Both shots hit nothing but net.

After the game Coach took Jordi and me to see Cooper in the hospital. Everyone else went back on the bus. Cooper had suffered a concussion. The doctor strongly advised him to stay overnight to see the results of a test, but he insisted on going home with us. He noticeably slurred his speech. His hand shook a little, too. When we offered to call his dad, he said fiercely that he didn't want that either. He just *had* to go home. If we didn't take him with us, he warned, he'd sneak out and find his own way back to Philo. Since we had to drive through there as it was, Coach agreed with the proviso that he tell his dad what happened and they find out about the test results in the morning.

I sat next to Coop in the back of Coach's Buick as we drove the winding roads toward the coast. He hardly said a word the entire time. He just stared at the seat in front of him. Occasionally, we tried to engage him in talk about the game or the state tournament, but for the most part we ended up letting him be as usual.

One time, when conversation died down and Coach had turned on the radio, I quietly asked, "Are you all right, Coop?" He looked at a folded up piece of paper on his lap, which he turned over with nervous fingers, rehearsing various answers to the question in his head, but he said nothing.

Not long after that we came to Philo, a little town composed of a lumber mill, a general store, and a few houses. Coach slowed down, but Coop asked if we could drop him off a little further along the road. We moved on, driving for a while in the total darkness of the countryside. Then Coop told us to stop. There weren't any lights except one or two windows set way back in the distance.

"You sure?" said Coach.

"I can walk from here."

We pulled over and he got out. Coach, Jordi, and I shot apprehensive looks at one another. I didn't want to leave him there alone. Coach, sensing he needed to do something, got out of the car and came around to the other side. I scooted after Coop, and Jordi, opening his door, stood up, too. Coach leaned against the side of the car and lit an Erik. We took in the scent of apples from an orchard that was sensed more than seen on the other side of a ditch.

"Whereabouts do you live around here, Coop?" asked Coach.

"Not far."

"We can take you all the way home, if you want."

"It's up a dirt road," he said. "It's pretty washed out this time of year."

"How come I've never met your dad, Coop?"

"He keeps to himself, I guess."

Coach absorbed that with a questioning silence. He took a drag on his cigarette. He was unsure how far to push this. "Maybe we ought to talk about what happened tonight," he said then. "You, me, and your dad, I mean."

Coop didn't want this to happen. "It's pretty late. He's most likely asleep by now."

Coach saw the sense in that. I could see him talking himself out of whatever funny qualms he had. "Damn, it's cold out here." He hesitated a few seconds more, settling against more interference. He threw his cigarette in the ditch. "Let's get this show on the road."

He walked back around the car as Coop started down the shoulder in the opposite direction. From his open door Coach called out, "Hey, Coop!" He made what he said then seem casual, like an afterthought. "You tell your dad I want him to call me, okay? I want to talk to him."

Coop hardly paused to nod in reply, hurrying on into the night. Back in the car I found that folded up piece of paper on the seat. I opened it as we drove off and recognized the flier for that missing little boy I'd seen for the first time only a few days before, on Point Cabrillo.

§

Coop walked the two miles of that dirt road he lived on and crept up to the house. He hoped his father would be asleep, even though he saw the light in the kitchen window. Coop found him, instead, huddled by a cast-iron stove, awaiting his return. He asked about the game, and Coop told him we'd won. His father frowned. He was afraid of that.

Coop pulled a chair to the stove and warmed himself. His father told him he could have the leftovers from dinner that were in the refrigerator. Coop wasn't hungry. Neither had much to say after that, but they kept it up for lack of anything better to do. They had to talk around the little boy who lay drugged with sleeping pills in the next room.

Coop had come to a decision after he cracked his skull against the wall in Ukiah. It had been tormenting him since the day his father brought the boy home, along with the fear of what his father would do if he found out what he had in mind. Simple logistics proved daunting enough to muffle his resolve. His father never left the boy alone and hardly ever slept when Coop was around, probably because he already anticipated treachery of some kind. So Coop had to act, when he did, with as much foresight and cunning as he could muster, and he didn't know how much of either he had. What they boiled down to so far was giving no sign of his intentions, which meant going about his own life as he normally would. He had a hard time seeing how that differed from making no decision at all.

That night Coop's problems came pressing in on him. He lived in fear of his father. It gripped from deep in his past with an almost unearthly strength. He couldn't do anything without running it through the filter of his father's suspicion. He had to watch himself the way he was watched, and it had been going on for so long it was second nature to him. He felt like stunned prey in his father's spidery midst, slowly eaten alive.

He'd gotten used to this permanent draining away of blood and spirit. He hardly knew anything else. It formed a routine he kept up with himself, binding him ever more tightly to his father with each adaptation he made, each victory won against his fear. And the more balance he learned to maintain this way, the more strangely he felt linked to the man. He even felt a kind of responsibility for him. They'd become collaborators in self-preservation. Two outlaws hiding out.

This responsibility also worked the other way. His father wasn't entirely heartless. He'd cared for Coop in his fashion. He'd given him what he could, and he'd even changed his usual secretive habits so Coop might enjoy some part of a normal kid's life. That's why he allowed him to play basketball, even though the risks he was always calculating rose accordingly. But he'd made Coop agree that, in order to keep playing, he would have to make some sort of excuse and bow out if the team won a berth in the state tournament. It was one thing to be seen in little towns in the middle of nowhere, but quite another to be seen in front of who knew how many people in Sacramento. That was too much exposure for so private a man as his father, and especially now.

The problem was Coop needed something like the state tournament, the way it accounted for his whereabouts and time, if he expected to catch his father enough at unawares to slip off with the boy. There was no other option. He had to force his father into changing his mind. To do that, he had to draw on the memory of another barely remembered self—not Coop, the scared and taciturn Mendocino teenager, but someone named Josh Hamilton, the kid who once got into a car with a strange man in Klamath Falls, Oregon, never to be seen again.

I didn't put these things together in my mind right away, or if I did, I couldn't believe what that man sketched on the sheet of paper might mean for Coop. But it left me uneasy enough to wonder. He showed up for the next practice, trying hard to act as if nothing out of the ordinary had happened. He said the doctor had told him he was fine, but you could tell he wasn't fine on the court. His instincts were off. I saw him try to hide the fact, even to himself. Coach went easy on him, but he was worried enough to call the doctor in Ukiah and find out that Coop's concussion warranted complete rest and no play, at least for the week leading up to the state tournament. Coach benched him during practice.

At the same time Coop had to tell Coach that his father didn't want him in Sacramento. He pleaded for Coach to intercede on his behalf after practice one evening, glossing his desperation as a desire to play. Coach agreed to call right from the little office in the locker room. Just before he did, Coop blurted out that his father didn't know about the head injury.

"Isn't that why he doesn't want you to play?"

"No. He needs me at home. To take care of things while he's at work."

That sounded like a lie. If Coach hadn't wanted Coop on the team for his own reasons, it might even have been enough for him to wash his hands of the whole situation. But he went ahead and called his father, who didn't answer the phone. Coop then urged him to come to his house and talk to his father in person. This was a demanding request from a guy who never asked for anything. It added still more incentive for Coach to agree.

He drove out there with Jordi and me the next morning, a Saturday. The dirt road switched back up a hillside. The house stood in a stand of fir trees, plunged all day long in gloom. Coop had told his father about the visit, so he greeted us with as much composure as he had in him. He still seemed jumpy, though, and Coach made the case for Coop's importance to the team with a directness that unnerved the man even more.

He had the same problem Coop did giving reasons why his son shouldn't go to Sacramento. It was clear just looking around the house that nothing needed to be cared for. His dad's insistence was unusual enough to raise other kinds of suspicions, too. He must have felt the risk in that because he agreed in the end, just as Coop hoped he would. His plan worked.

Coach spent a lot of time in those days before the state tournament talking on the phone to people from all over the country about Chase. Some of them even made the trip to Mendocino. They were successful people who were savvy about basketball, and Coach felt part of a world where he belonged. One coach had even invited him to take part in trials for a high school all-star team that would compete nationally that summer.

Meanwhile, the ex-teammate from his Oklahoma days lobbied for him at Stanford. It may have been a long shot, but no matter. Even if he didn't get the job, he had his heart set on somewhere far away from little towns and thwarted hopes. He'd been broken down for a long time, and too caught in his own mistakes to do much else than turn resignation into a virtue. That didn't come naturally to anyone, but it was particularly hard for Coach to bottle up his emotions like that. He'd grown tired of seeing life as a penance. Maybe there was still time for a second chance.

Of course, chance can be fluky and swing in any number of directions. You can't count on it. I tended to worry for this reason among others.

Sky broke up with Fox only a few days before we left for Sacramento. It plunged him back into his moody fatalism. I went out with him and Zach the same night, hoping to keep them from driving into a ditch and killing themselves. They clearly intended to get as wasted as possible, no matter what Coach might say the next day. We ended up after midnight lying in the bed of Fox's truck on a mesa of scrub pine outside of town. It was a place where people liked to race their cars along the miles of empty back roads.

We stared up at the stars. I pretended to drink my beer while they went methodically through the rest of the case they'd bought. Fox tried to persuade us he'd never again find anyone as "good to fuck" as Sky. Zach didn't help by cutting in every now and then with a "She *is* outrageously hot" or "Girls like that *are* once in a lifetime," adding depth to Fox's gloom.

Zach could be a little insensitive. You had the feeling sometimes that not much concerned him. I wouldn't call it cynicism. He simply had next to no idea of those lower registers in the soul where Fox could sink like a shipwreck on the sea floor, and so reassuring someone who did just didn't occur to him. Zach went along for the ride, admiring the scenery as it rolled by and thinking there always had to be more stops before you got to the end. You admired him for that, too.

I took my fill of the night while they went on talking in this vein. It was incredibly clear. The sky was etched with stars. Zach made me laugh when he observed, stating the obvious, "You can see the galaxy, man."

This jarred Fox into searching the night for what Zach meant by that. In all likelihood he only saw the structures of his own doom, but the effort settled him down. That sky did make your problems seem kind of small.

"I wonder what Sky's doing right now," Fox said.

"Probably fucking some other guy," said Zach dreamily.

"Damn, Zach!" I broke out, regretting it the same instant.

"What?"

Keeping my secret about Sky, I had no ready answer. I seized on the first lame thing that popped into my head: "I'm drunk."

Fox, meanwhile, had retreated back into his hole so completely that he missed any anomaly in the moment. With a sudden jerk of his arm he threw his empty beer can as far over the side as he could, where it landed in the brush. The sound met the ear in a nice feathery way. The contrast it made with his aggression pissed him off even more.

"I'm drunk off my ass!" he yelled into the night. "Drunk off my stupid pig-fucking redneck ass!"

"Fuck yeah!" said Zach, as if he agreed, throwing his can and listening while it sailed through the air for the same feathery sound. He liked it more than Fox did.

All Suzanne could talk about in those days was the seismic survey and how upset it had made her—enough, she said, to change all her plans and become an environmental activist. She spoke about moving to San Francisco instead of LA and getting involved with groups there. I wondered from this if she might also want to be close to Chase in Palo Alto, if that's where he ended up going, but she never mentioned it. She had a mind of her own, whatever happened.

I didn't have the nerve to ask Chase about Sky, but he brought it up himself the day before we left for Sacramento. He gave me a lift home after practice and told me outside my house that he wasn't seeing her anymore, "in case you were wondering."

Over the discomfort that whole affair could still rouse in me, I said, "I hope it works out between you."

"We'll see. Most of the time these days we just fight."

My mother had appeared in our yard, moving the dogs around in the expectation of me helping her get them into cages for the night. It was dusk, but Chase could see she wore a mask over her face to protect her from the dander.

"What's wrong with your mom?"

"She has emphysema."

He stared back at me, astonished. "Why didn't you tell me?"

"I don't know," I said with a shrug. "It never came up."

He decided against responding to the hurt I frankly didn't much feel like hiding. "Is she all right?"

"She takes it a day at a time."

He looked off toward the trailer park, wanting for some reason to draw the moment out. I think he felt bad about how things had ended between us. We weren't friends anymore. "Ready for tomorrow?" he asked.

"As I'll ever be."

"I think we're going to win." He drew a breath before adding, in as sincere a tone as I'd ever heard from him: "Everybody's going to win."

That confidence, and his good intentions, stayed with me until the next morning. We had to be in front of the gym at the crack of dawn with our suitcases packed. A lot of other people showed up, too, as the school had arranged a second bus for fans who wanted to support us. Half the town must have been there to see us off. It turned into an impromptu pep rally.

As we headed off, Zach started clapping, and people joined in one by one. The tempo increased with the volume. Zach introduced a few polyrhythms into the mix with the help of a tire iron he'd fished out of the bus tool kit and banged on the chrome bar that rimmed the seat in front of him. Pretty soon others were thwacking at windows or stomping their feet. Even Coach, sitting up front next to the net bag full of basketballs, got into it.

As we rolled out of town toward Fort Bragg and the road that would take us inland, we worked ourselves up to a frenzied pitch by chanting over long intervals the syllables, "*Men—do—ci—no! Men—do—ci—no!*" over and over again. We were still at it when we passed Point Cabrillo. A view opened over sloping fields to the trailer park in the middle distance. I also caught, way back down the headlands by the sea, just the faintest glimmer from the lighthouse lens.

For some reason its simple anachronistic signal didn't comfort me. I felt, in fact, more unease than anything. We were going out into a world of messages more complex and coded than any of us had experienced before. How would we be able to keep track of them, or track ourselves by them, when we were used to living by lighthouses? It was then that I noticed Coop hadn't gotten on the bus.

15

We checked into the motel in Sacramento that afternoon and rested up for a couple of hours before we left for the arena. Soon Coach came into the room Jordi and I shared and told us to turn on the television. To our shock, nearly every channel had reports going about Cooper and the little boy. Coach told Jordi to get everybody else in there. Slowly, they all filed through the doorway to hear the news.

Early that morning Coop's father had driven him to Mendocino and dropped him off by the high school. He wanted to see him actually get on that bus with the rest of us, but when he saw the press of cars and people spilling out of the parking lot in front of the gym, he decided to let Coop walk in by himself. He did wait around until the busses left. Someone would claim later to have seen him loitering outside the high school.

Coop had passed through the parking lot and back into the main building, where he waited until he knew we were gone and his father would've most likely headed back home. To make sure he wasn't observed, Coop walked with his duffel bag of clothes almost a mile in the opposite direction before he started hitchhiking. He caught a ride that took him to the same spot where we'd dropped him off with Coach. But he didn't walk on the dirt road. He bushwhacked up steep wooded slopes to the ridge where he lived and hid within view of the house, where he saw his father's car parked out front.

He expected to wait who knew how long before his father went out again. He'd brought some food and a blanket, in case it was all night. Since the boy had arrived, his father kept up a ceaseless vigil in the house. He laid low even when Coop went to school. If he needed supplies, he took the boy with him, drugged on sleeping pills and dead to the world on the back seat.

Coop didn't have long to wait, however. As he suspected would eventually happen, his father went into Boonville to eat in the café where I'd met him that one time. He planned to stay awhile, so it made no sense to leave the boy alone in the car. He locked the boy inside the house for the second time that day and drove off.

Coop waited long enough to make sure he was right about the meal in Boonville, then he broke into the house and, lifting the doped up boy from his bed, left back down the hill through the woods. Never before had Coop needed the strength that had gradually changed him from the child he used to be, the one so afraid of his father that still he quaked before him, into the man who could carry that boy as far as the highway. The head injury must have made it that much harder.

Again he hitched a ride, this time with a logging truck. The driver asked if anything was wrong with the boy. Coop made up some story about a sleep disorder they were treating with drugs. He took no chances with anybody. The driver dropped them off at the turn for the road to Ukiah, just past Boonville. As the truck rumbled through the center of town, Coop shrank back against the seat. His father's car was parked in front of the café.

The boy had come out of his stupor as they stood on the side of the highway. He cried silent tears but asked no questions after Coop said, "I'm taking you home." They hardly spoke after that. He could see in the boy the complete docility that comes over you when terror strikes deep into the heart. No reasons would ever be able to account for why you just went along, why you didn't run or fight or cry. Coop knew you just tried to conserve your energy.

He arrived in Ukiah while it was still morning and surprised everybody at the courthouse by announcing what he'd done. The news broke right away, and inside of an hour journalists from all over the state began arriving to report the dramatic rescue of the kidnapped boy. Not the least sensational aspect of the story, of course, would be the discovery that his rescuer had been kidnapped in just the same way, twelve years before.

⁙

The man Coop called his father would figure out what happened the instant he found the boy gone. He fled, keeping to back roads as much as possible until nightfall. By then, not only the police but the forest service and the DEA were on alert. Even under cover of darkness it didn't take them long to spot him on the remote highway to Manchester. There they trapped him in a grove of redwood trees after he drove his car into a ditch and tried to escape on foot. The next day it was announced that he'd been captured.

It turned out the man had once before been convicted of child kidnapping in Idaho and spent seven years in prison as a result. He had also been charged with sexual molestation at the time, and people were relieved now to find out from doctors who examined the little boy that no evidence in this direction had been found. Josh Hamilton, however, would reveal that he'd been routinely sodomized since he was six until only last year. It appeared he'd grown too old to be of interest anymore to the man.

That shook us all up. We felt the sudden end of our own youth in that hotel room as it took one decisive step out of innocence. It was like opening a window in time. The many years of knowing each other revealed, in the changed light, a strangeness we had never suspected, or worse, did suspect and never admitted to ourselves. The awful clarity of this shift left us cautious, even downright mistrustful, with one another. We had touched each other over the years in ways sullied now by a desire not to know. We felt both victimized and guilty. A specter of pure prejudice appeared among us in that room, conjured out of a violation between men and boys that we sensed had no bottom or limit. It reached so personally inside us that it might have broken every bond of fellowship we had.

Coach sensed the delicacy of the moment and how carefully those bonds might need to be remade if we were to go out on that court and play another game of basketball. He had to be completely candid. With this in mind, he began talking about manhood and what it meant to take responsibility for yourself in a world that cut into the flesh, left scars, and healed up around your own flaws.

"I've made a hash of it myself," he conceded. "I won't pretend otherwise. I'm a sonofabitch most of the time, you know that. I've been so full of hate and self-pity I wanted to choke. It almost killed me." The confessional tone in his voice wavered here. I could see his eyes wandering into the past. Jordi leaned gravely against one wall. I thought of Terry muttering on the beach that day I first saw her in town.

Coach picked up his theme on another register. "I've been in the army and I've been in prison," he went on. "I've seen just what men will do given half a chance. I don't see any point in denying it. They break you. They break you all the way down if they can. And when that's true, the only choice you have is to fight. That's what this game, this whole season, is about for me. Teaching you how to fight—"

"You don't *always* have to fight," Chase said in a low voice.

"The hell you don't," Coach snapped. "That just tells me you're used to other people doing the fighting for you." He regretted the heat in his response, turning it down again degree by degree. "But it doesn't matter. The point is we come from different places. Mine isn't the only one. I'm not a wise man. I never much cared for those who claimed they were. I only know what it's like to come from a particular place and own up to that."

Fox and Zach had slipped silently into the room during this exchange. I hadn't even realized they were absent. Fox's face looked as pale and drawn as a man frozen in ice. I assumed they'd heard about Cooper on their own.

"I'll just speak for myself then," Coach said. "I'll tell you what I think I do know. In this world, there's winners and losers, with nothing in between. There's people who break you down and people who are broken down. I know that sounds harsh, but it's what I've seen from where I stand. And if I know what it takes to be a winner, it's only because I've lost. Hell, I've been a loser all my life. I know winning from the other side, looking in, like a one-eyed cat at the seafood store. I was set up to lose. And what I had to find out is that the set-up works in the mind, where you think about who and what you are. That's where all the hurting really starts. It's also where you have to fight first. The *mental* fight. That's what we all need to be doing right now. We can't let what's happened to Coop psyche us out. It's too important. It's a lesson you've got to learn one way or another. If you learn it now, it'll be a lot sooner than I did."

At that point Jordi solemnly interjected, "Let's do it for Coop." We turned toward him, and he saw the thought form in all our minds of him taking over at the forward position. It made me mad that it had to be a thought of weakness, a worry, which he also took in because he added, "I'll do my best anyway."

"You all will," said Coach. "Play your hearts out and the rest sort of takes care of itself."

He got up and turned off the television, ordering us back to our rooms until it was time to go. As we broke up, I saw Fox deliberately avoid looking anybody in the eye as he walked out the door. That worried me. I slid over to Zach. "What's wrong?" I whispered.

"Nothing," he told me. Fox had just been talking to Sky.

Chase didn't tell me what Sky thought of them no longer seeing each other. I only found out later that she'd come over to his house the night before the tournament when Suzanne was there, after repeatedly calling a phone he'd judiciously left off the hook for the evening. She'd been volatile like this since he explained to her that he didn't want a serious relationship. He thought she would understand that, but his glamor had worked a spell upon her deeper aspirations that someone without small town insecurities might miss easily enough. We come from different places, as Coach had said, but we also assume that every place is the same, and everyone is the same, too. This tends to drive the differences down into shadows that hide us even from ourselves.

That night before the tournament, Sky worked herself into an infatuated panic with the help of the key she'd stolen to her stepfather's liquor cabinet. She could hardly keep the car on the road by the time she left for Point Cabrillo. Chase and Suzanne awoke to the sound of her banging on the front door and screaming into the night.

"Who's that?" Suzanne said, her heart gearing down this steep hill of catastrophe.

"I don't know." He slid out of bed and put on a pair of shorts. "Stay here."

He went downstairs as apprehensive as he was annoyed. When he opened the door, he found Sky holding up a screwdriver as if she meant to stab him with it. He took this in at a glance, along with her hectic hair, her desperate eyes, and the idling car canted in the middle of the road behind her. The swooning glare from the lens in the lighthouse seemed accelerated like the dopplered light of police sirens. "What are you doing?" he asked as calmly as he could.

"You wouldn't answer!" she cried.

He didn't try to excuse himself. "I can't talk right now."

"Why not?"

"You know why."

"No, I don't!"

"My girlfriend's here."

She brought the screwdriver down in a sudden arc. Chase leapt back, but not before it glanced his chest and tore open the flesh over the ribcage. "Jesus Christ, Sky!"

She stumbled and fell onto the porch. He took the screwdriver from her hand and propped her up against the side of the house. Then he went in to wash off the blood that had welled into the gash on his chest. When he came back, he crouched beside her and thought about what to do next.

"You're hurt," she simpered.

He took this in with a frown, noticing her opened blouse and nearly exposed breasts.

"You're a mess," he said, buttoning it up.

"I love you."

A sardonic gleam came into his eyes. "That's because you don't know me." He spoke more to himself. It was clear she wouldn't remember anything in the morning.

"My mouth is dry," she said irrelevantly.

"You have to leave," he told her, seeing at the same time how impossible this would be in her present state. There'd be no way around a confrontation with Suzanne. He tried to stand her up. "Come on."

"Where are we going?"

"You can crash on the couch."

As he helped her through the front door, he saw Suzanne descending the stairs, dressed with her things in the bag she'd brought. She had completed the puzzle from the bedroom. If she hadn't, Sky furnished the final piece by sizing her up with a rival's eye and asking Chase, "Why can't I sleep with you?"

The way Suzanne ignored this made Sky feel distinctly petty and small. In the sort of games she played with other girls, it stripped her of any advantage. She leaned more heavily on Chase, but it made no difference; she was the stranger in that moment. They all knew it.

Suzanne meant to walk by without a word, but she noticed the gash and that brought her up short. She decided against asking if he was okay. "Why am I not surprised, Chase?"

He could only stand helplessly by while she plumbed the depth of the long silence that passed between them.

"That's just the way things are, huh?" She offered this more as a remark than a question. He admired its tactical quality.

"For right now," he had to say.

"You do what you do anyway, right?"

He had that coming, too. "I guess so."

"Go to hell," she said, turning on her heel and walking out the door.

⚡

Sky woke up the next day alone in Chase's house—his father had been on his research vessel at sea the whole time. She found a note from Chase that said simply, "Thanks for fucking everything up." These words ran through her mind on the drive home, intensifying the sense of her own insignificance in his eyes. It was humiliating, and she responded by pulling back into what she knew, into the power she still did have to reaffirm her pride. When she called Zach's cell phone later and got Fox on the line, it was with little consciousness of spite that she told him Chase and her had been sleeping together for weeks.

It may have been that the anger Fox felt on hearing this would not, by itself, have been enough to pitch him over an edge. It needed the news about Coop and Coach's speech on the feeling of violation that ran right to the most sensitive core of a masculine being. All of this together kept him and Zach quiet while the team drove to the arena and dispersed into the cavernous stands for the first half of the game before ours.

I saw the two of them seated way up at the top row by the roof. No one was around them because the arena was only half-full at the time. I sat nearer to the court with Jordi, who took copious notes on the game for his dad. We'd have to play the winner if we made it past the first round. If not, we'd pack it up and head home—there'd be no other chance.

Coach was seated with his friend from Stanford on the other side of the court. From their animated conversation I guessed they were reminiscing about old times. Chase sat down and over from us about ten rows. As I watched, he left his seat and descended the aisle toward the floor, disappearing under a concrete overhang to the locker rooms where we'd left our stuff. When I looked up at that top row again, Fox and Zach were gone.

They found Chase a few minutes later in the bathroom, redressing the bandage on his chest. He caught sight of Fox in the mirror just as Fox hammered him over the head with the tire iron he'd taken from the bus and stashed inside his coat. Chase's knees buckled under him, and he collapsed over the sink with a cry that was cut brutally short as his chin banged the porcelain rim. He sprawled in a heap on the floor.

"Jesus!" cried Zach, who hadn't known about the tire iron. To his horror, Fox raised it above his head a second time. Zach lunged at it. He pulled back Fox's arm and, after a struggle, wrested the tire iron from him.

"Are you crazy?" He stared a few long, breathless seconds into Fox's eyes, seeing there something more terrible than he had ever noticed before. It rattled him, that proof of his own heedlessness, and all he could say was, "Not with this."

Fox then set about kicking Chase with his pointy boot and jabbing at him with the heel, while Zach retreated to the bathroom door and kept watch over the adjoining hallway. He must have wondered, in the turn of events, how easily a person might mistake fucking up for principle, complicity for friendship. They might even have been the same thing, only right then that didn't sit so well with him. Disaster could just become *your* disaster in the end, and you had to live with that.

Fox, meanwhile, venting his fury on Chase, preoccupied with betrayal and vengeance and lust, too, must at some level have hit on the same idea. I like to think it came to him as a memory from his childhood, one he'd told me about a long time before. He was five. There'd been a cold spell unlike any those coastal ranges had seen in a generation, and the pond where we often went swimming in the summer had frozen over, solidly enough for a year-old calf to wander out onto it. But the ice wouldn't support the weight of a man, or even that of the calf, for very long, and they had to lure it back from the bank. Fox looked on as the calf grew more confused and frightened. Everything became very distinct in his senses then, as isolated and precarious as that petrified animal. When the ice at last broke under its hooves and it collapsed into the water, he could feel some part of himself giving way, too, kicking helplessly while the solid world melted around him, and all that remained was slow drowning.

❧

They dragged Chase into a bathroom stall and left him crumpled on the floor. As he regained his senses, he heard the team currently playing come in for halftime. He pulled himself onto the toilet, daubed his bloodied lip and nose, and waited until they were gone.

Shortly after that, we arrived to start suiting up. Chase came out and stood before the bathroom mirror to pick up where he'd left off redressing the gash. Coach walked by and saw him still in his clothes.

"Get your ass in there," he ordered.

Chase ignored him, carefully stretching a bandage over the skin on his chest and trying hard to keep steady over his feet. Coach, noticing this, came close enough to see his face in the mirror. "Jesus!" he cried. When Chase ignored this, too, Coach grabbed him by the shoulder and pulled him into the locker room.

"What happened to Chase?" he demanded of us.

We stared horrified at the livid bruises on his cheeks, the split lip, the cut across his forehead. I glanced from Fox to Zach. Both of them solemnly laced their shoes.

Coach lunged at Fox and yanked him up from the bench, drilling holes into his impassive face. "Who did this?"

Fox replied, "I did."

"Why?"

Fox looked away rather than answer. Coach shoved him, and he fell back between the bench and a locker. "What the hell is going on?"

His eyes prowled around the room. No one dared to speak. Meanwhile, Chase had begun suiting up. Seeing this, Coach swung over to his own bag and fished out a first aid kit. He ordered Chase to sit down as he soaked a disinfectant in gauze. He raised the gauze to Chase's face.

"I'm all right," Chase mumbled, chewing on his words through the pain in his jaw.

"No, you're not."

"*I can play!*" he screamed, yanking his arm free from Coach's grip. He glared malevolently at all of us, fighting back tears. "I'm going to fucking play."

The game passed like a nightmare. Aside from our own meltdown, we had trouble feeling our way in that vast arena, which was still half empty despite what must have been thousands of onlookers. We felt more exposed than we had in our lives and yet as lost in equivalence as a grain of sand. It was hard to believe we were there at all, and the awe in that brought to our feet and hands, our breath, our balance, a numbness that made assessing distance and relation difficult. The basket looked so close we might shoot from anywhere and nail it, but it could also recede before the simplest lay-up. No touch seemed enough to calibrate the forces. The ball banged off the backboard or hit nothing but air. Our legs shot off from under us, yet running felt as slow as molasses. We were always trying to match up with ourselves.

We might have adjusted to the differences in scale with each other's help. We might have met the challenge of Coach's game one more time, with its innate respect for the accidental and the unexpected, and found the poise we needed. His game leaned into adversity, after all. It knew what grace could be woven out of error.

Instead, we refused to find each other. Fox looked right through Chase on the court, passing the ball anywhere but to him. Zach ran around like a chicken with his head cut off, wishing he could sneak off and smoke a joint. Chase went up against double and triple teams as if he were alone, like a soldier in the middle of a rout. Only Jordi and I sensed a center, a chance at pattern. Every time the chance was lost we tried to rally, to hold on in the breach.

Coach ran up and down the sideline, growing more furious by the minute. He snarled orders, worried the towel in his hands, and threw up his arms in disgust. I felt responsible for that unraveling, but Jordi bore it up like a cross on the road to Calvary.

The other team, from a town in the Central Valley, caught on soon enough to our utter disarray, slowing the tempo and executing well-ordered plays as if they knew exactly how to take us even further out of our game. Their coach sat on the bench, dressed in a proper suit with a shock of silver hair, dissecting us with steely blue eyes. He could not have presented more of a contrast: where Coach exploded, he withdrew into himself and waited, like a spider in his hole. If the man smelled blood, he didn't show it.

As the game went on, his nerveless self-control seeped over the entire floor. It seemed that way to me, at any rate, as I slowly lost my purchase in the moment. The game hovered before my eyes like afterimages on color fields. I heard it like the hiss of siphoned gas. Well before it was over, the pressure had become unbearable, and all I could think about was getting the hell out of there.

That pressure let up only in the last minutes, when the other team ran an inbounds play exactly like one of ours. It had their best player come off a pick and turn an alley oop pass from the top of the key into a hard dunk over the backs of Fox and Jordi.

With that their coach relaxed. A smirk creased his lips as he glanced at an assistant and then up the sideline at Coach, who jackknifed a water bottle back behind our bench and sat, covering his face with his hands. When he dropped them again, his eyes were haggard and bloodshot, fixed on nothing at all. He stayed like this until the final horn sounded. So our season came to an end.

16

Coach didn't return to the locker room afterward. We showered and dressed, no one talking to anyone else, too tired to fight or hate or care anymore. The high school principal appeared. He was as surprised as we were by Coach's absence. He walked with us to the bus, where we settled into our own worlds again while he went looking for Coach. It must have been half an hour before the principal returned to tell us with some embarrassment that Coach wouldn't be going back with us.

Jordi demanded to know where his father was, and the principal vaguely suggested he'd driven home with a friend. When Jordi refused to believe that and tried to get off the bus, he admitted no one knew where Coach was. He'd vanished from the arena. We went back to the motel for the night, hoping he'd turn up there, but he didn't. The next morning, we returned to Mendocino alone.

Coach wandered for a long time afterward through the streets of Sacramento, stuck inside himself. Once again he had to fight, and the terrain would have to be in his own mind, like he'd told us, where that fight had been going on for as long as he could remember, tearing at him like those dust bowl winds of his childhood. If he hadn't learned to defend himself then, there would have been no Ray Ellis careening through Sacramento into time and loss. It made him sharp and hard on the outside. Inside, it left him sensitive to the smallest slights, tender at the center like the flesh of prickly pears. He knew this about himself. Too much time and too much loss had sorted out the parts and he just had to lump it. Grow new thorns.

Later that night he walked into a bar on a commercial strip without exactly knowing why, the way you do when the scene shifts all at once in a dream. He made no excuses for the first shot of whiskey. After the second, risk receded past caring. He saw a pro basketball game at Madison Square Garden on a television fixed into the wall. He took that to be a bad omen. It reminded him of how little chance there really was in chance, which called for still another shot. He watched the game.

"I played on that floor once," he told the bartender. "*That* floor there. The Garden. I scored 35 points." He sensed a woman seated two stools down was listening to him as well. "Everything I threw up found the hole," he added slyly.

"Is that a fact?" said the bartender.

"The motherfuckers never knew what hit them."

Innuendo felt good. He decided to buy himself a bottle. The floor bowed beneath him as he took it, but it didn't make any difference now. Soon he was pouring one shot after the other. Each went down more smooth than the last, filling out the space in his head with a buzz twelve long years in the making. He tried to ignore the woman whose continuing interest shamed him. She wore a red satin dress with low cleavage, garnished with a carnation, along with horn-rimmed glasses and a frilly picture hat. Her face was made up in a style of exaggerated femininity, with glossy red lips to match her red hair. She was drunk, too.

"Hey, honey," she said. "Let up on the liquor."

"Mind your own business."

The woman nodded as she moved over a stool and tried to take the bottle away.

"Sure," she said. "Take a break on the shots, though, okay?"

"*Leave me alone!*" he barked, grabbing the bottle by the neck and walking down to the other end of the bar. He added over his shoulder, "I don't need no advice."

"I was just trying to help," she called out.

"I don't need your help."

"Suit yourself. Sorry I bothered."

He eyed her sideways in his peripheral vision, while he also tried to watch the game from the new angle. His thoughts combined into more and more deadly obsession. "Don't need any help from the likes of you," he said presently. "Got all the help I needed a long time ago." He mimicked a nagging woman's voice. "'Stop drinking, Ray. It's killing you.' Shit!" he said, pitching his voice to a growl of accusation. "Stop the knife they got twisting in my gut first, you stupid bitch!"

This outburst worried the bartender. "You okay, mister?"

He stared. "Sure, I'm okay. Never felt better." He was getting into the swing of things now. "Got me some *woman* trouble, that's all," he said, with a nod at the redhead.

Eventually the bar closed and he found himself on his own again. He thought about getting back to the motel, but he couldn't for the life of him recall where it was. He walked through the streets, huddled for warmth in the creased blazer he wore during the game. He came at last to a late night liquor store, where he bought another bottle of whiskey and a pack of Eriks. On the way out he passed a Chinese man who'd left a beat up Toyota running on the street out front. Coach looked incredulously back through the glass storefront, and then he crouched to see that the keys really did dangle from the ignition. He craned his neck up and down the deserted street. Everything seemed to be telling him to go, so he got into the car and took off as naturally as if it belonged to him.

He drove around Sacramento feeling euphoric. His fingertips just grazed the steering wheel while he took swigs from the bottle. His eyes were fugitive gleams skittering off side and rear view mirrors. He hoped to hit upon the motel with the same good luck that had landed him the car, but it didn't happen, and by dawn the aimless circling had stopped being fun. He checked into another motel and passed out until the middle of the next day.

He awoke sober enough to conceive of getting back to Mendocino, so he headed north on the interstate as far as the turn off for Highway 20, which would take him all the way to Fort Bragg. By then, however, he'd started with the liquor again. As night set in over the hills, he wondered if he was going to make it. He had to drive so carefully that other cars and trucks backed up behind him. He pulled over and got out until later, when he'd have the road more to himself.

He walked into a field that sloped up to a ravine clotted with oak trees. He headed to a serpentine outcropping and sat drinking in the loneliness of the spot. No simple vagary had brought him there. The damp, the smell of grass, the cicadas, the flick of bat wings, the gnomic signaling of owls—it all ran him straight into the traps of his life, laid way back in immemorial beginnings. "I'm nothing but white trash," he declared to the night. "A fucking Okie."

Once he beat up a man for calling him that in a bar in Barstow, while on leave from the nearby army base. He was drunk and the man had said it in the wrong way, and he stuck a broken bottle in the man's face to make sure he understood how he felt about it. But the spending of his rage, or the taking of revenge, was subject to the same chemistry as alcohol in the brain: you needed more and more to get the same feeling, until nothing was too much.

It seemed as if he'd slipped through a crack in the world. No one knew where he was and that meant he was accountable to no one. Anything he did was okay. There were no witnesses. To be outside the consideration of others like this had its appeal. Nothing opposed him. From absence of constraint came victory over weight and gravity. Later, driving again, he experimented with this freedom by sliding over into the opposite lane around blind turns. He shut off his headlights and drove in darkness on a straightaway. The night shattered all his bulk. He was completely himself, a law among laws.

Of course, the first close call with an oncoming car was enough to remind him of the risks he was taking. He may have been that sovereign person in one respect, but he was also mortal, a thing, outside the world. This double fact enraged him. He felt its ghostly shiver down his spine. He felt it freeze each vertebra into a visceral hatred. That was the one true emotion he'd maybe ever had. It might consume him. He might choke on it. But it connected him to this thing he was in the darkness, to its refusal and revolt.

The road rose gradually into highlands, following ridgelines and opening onto moonlit vistas. It seemed like he was gaining perspective even as his thoughts grew more fantastic in his mind. He saw that every attempt to be someone— husband, father, player, coach—flickered back into being no one at all. The difference was a promise he'd been chasing his whole life. But the promise was a lie, he understood now, and the lie had no beginning or end. Its place was only ever the present, this passing through the night devoured in his headlights. *I am the lie. I am the emptiness of all promises.* Hence that simple preference in him for flaring out, like a meteorite in atmosphere. He'd rather burn than smolder and smoke. He'd rather force his own nullity into the open than huddle in other people's sense of the good, pretending he wasn't the sonofabitch he'd always been. So what if he was? So what if it only confirmed every prejudice, every judgment, every goddamn evil thought anyone had ever had of him? Sometimes you had to fight fire with fire.

The next day, white-knuckling it past a caravan of RVs just outside Clear Lake, he felt his engine cut out on him. He glanced at the pointer on the fuel gauge, stuck on empty, and felt all momentum drain away while he maneuvered the car to a dead stop on the side of the road. One by one the RVs passed him by again.

He got out and walked down the highway, thinking about edges. He'd never escaped them no matter how hard he tried. At the edge, over the edge, in the edge, it hardly mattered. He'd always been standing on the edges of events that didn't include him. He was the coach on the sideline, the drunk in the ditch, the bent back in a potato field, the star on the court who felt so edgy he could barely stand it. *Shit.* He swerved over to a gap in the pine trees that lined that part of the highway and looked defiantly over a gulch. At his feet on the other side of the rail guard, he found an almost intact skeleton of a deer, the flesh long since picked clean.

Later, on walking to a gas station, he bought a plastic container with two gallons of gas, lugged it back to the car, and got on the road again. He stopped at the next station and filled up his tank. Right before cradling the pump back in its berth, he decided to fill the plastic container a second time. He put it in the trunk, thinking *fight fire with fire, fight fire with fire.*

A few miles down the highway he stopped at another station and bought another container, telling the pump jockey the same story about running out. He may not have had a clear idea of a plan when he did this, since he was drinking the whole time and his actions ranged wide of his consciousness of them. But as he repeated the routine numerous times all the way past Willits, filling up the trunk, the seats, finally the whole cabin with plastic containers, he understood what he was aiming to do. It was simple: jump out of the edge and enter by force into the event.

He rolled into Mendocino toward nine o'clock and drove around the high school to the empty parking lot in front of the gym. He carried two containers at a time up the stairs and through the front door he'd opened with his key, piling them at center court. When he had them all in, he opened each one and poured the gasoline in lurid slicks over the floor. He had to concentrate. How did you burn down a gym anyway? *Start at the bottom.*

He carried a container downstairs to the men's locker room. He took all the towels he could find, soaked them, and left them strewn on benches, on top of lockers, in the small coach's office. He pulled the tarps off the old weightlifting equipment they kept in the back basement, right in the foundations of the building, and piled them one on top of the other, dousing them with more gasoline. He lit the pile with a match and watched it kindle like a bonfire. Then he emptied the container in wide arcs across the room, igniting the whole basement around him.

That had him leaping back through the flames to the locker room, where he started more fires with a rolled up newspaper. He inched toward the stairs as the space filled with a thick smoke. When it became too suffocating, he ran up to the court and pushed the other containers against the wall beneath the stage. He opened each one and retreated to the far side.

By the entrance he pulled an Erik out of his pack and lit it. After a couple of drags, he threw it as far into the gym as he could. When it landed the entire floor lit up, shimmering with the static insinuation of electric current. A moment later the containers opposite exploded with a force so intense it shattered the high paned windows. Fire rolled up into the rafters and flowed back down again, fighting with itself in the middle air.

Coach shrank into the vestibule, stunned both by the violence of it and by the sudden loss of control. He wondered if he was thinking clearly. Things weren't going the way he'd hoped. He was still where he'd always been: on the edge. He'd made a mistake.

In fact he'd gotten things exactly backward. It wasn't into the event that he had to go but *to its other side*, to its nether regions. This made more sense. He had to go back behind the world, back behind appearances to the real source of pain and failure, to the real place where the seeds of his life had been pulled, with the dirt, right out of the ground. He smiled craftily, took another swig of whiskey from the pint he kept in his back pocket, and left the gym.

The fire horn ripped through town. It climbed to a deafening pitch, then disintegrated in strange mournful decompression. I heard it from Point Cabrillo without thinking much of it, since they set it off for most any kind of emergency. But the blasts continued long enough to make me wonder.

Zach called to tell me the gym was on fire. A little later he came to pick me up. I didn't want to leave my mother without the van. Together, we drove to the high school.

I watched from the parking lot with a growing number of people. The gym was oddly intact, but the interior cooked like a wood stove at white heat. You could see fire eating away at the rafters through the high windows. Then the roof fell in, taking with it one whole corner of wall, and the released flames leapt into the night. Clearly, the gym was a lost cause. The real problem became the outlying trailers used as classrooms and the main building on the hill. The volunteer firemen formed a line on the intervening dirt slope, intent on containing the fire there.

A Coast Guard helicopter presently appeared. It eased over the gym and dumped more water. The scene took on a dream-like quality at this point. Everything seemed to be happening in slow motion: the massive hovering thing in the sky, swooning rotor wash, dopplered sirens, the hectic shadows thrown by firelight, the firefighters in their yellow coats and hoods making silhouettes against the glare.

The scene didn't arouse the same avidity in me that it did in Zach and others who stood nearby. They felt the pleasure kids take in seeing things explode, but their pleasure was darker and graver, more fascinated with destruction. My sense of the truth in this, and my own heartbroken feeling for the gym itself, closed out my interest altogether. I withdrew back through the crowd to the other end of the parking lot where I could look out over the headlands and the sea beyond. The beam of the lighthouse, two miles up the coast, swept through the night. Its synchronous flash penetrated right into the optic nerve.

I walked past the art center into town, farther and farther away until the commotion of the fire had contracted into nothing more than the faint tattoo of the helicopter in my ears. I ended up at the middle school and crossed the empty court to the bank of ice plant. There I lay back and breathed the night air in, detecting through acrid smoke the scent of alyssum from the nearby baseball field. I wanted the familiarity this brought, the lowering of tensions that had begun to pull me away from any simple belonging. But it wasn't working. That background conflagration burned more than the gym in me.

I gave up and decided to keep wandering instead. As I entered the street again, I saw a car, for some reason driven on the wrong side, coming toward me. I waited for it to pass. Then I noticed an arm extended down from the open window, hugging the door. Just above the wrist, barely visible in the light of a street lamp, was a tattoo in the shape of a screaming eagle.

"Coach!" I cried, but, swinging by, he ignored me. I watched as he steered the car unsteadily back to the other lane in time to round the corner. It took me only a second to remember that Terry lived on that street.

I broke into a run, slowing down when I saw the car in front of her saltbox house and Coach banging on the front door. Lights were on inside, but no one answered. Coach stepped back from the porch and almost lost his balance on the stair. From the cover of night I could see that he was drunk. He peered up at a second-storey window and at both corners, discovering, as I once had, the path that led down the side of the house. He vanished into it.

I came closer, unsure what to do next. I had a bad feeling about Coach's intentions, but I still felt reluctant to interfere. I didn't really know how close Coach and Terry were, or what kind of arrangement they'd come to with each other. It might have included talking from time to time, for all I knew. Thinking of the last time I'd butted into something that wasn't my business, I wanted to be certain of the situation before I acted.

Then I heard raised voices from inside the house. Alarmed, I went to the porch, catching Coach's growl and snatches of words: "don't give a shit," "dragging on my ass," "like a whipped dog."

Terry replied as calmly as she could, but I could tell she was afraid. I also heard another man's pleading tones. It was Jordi. I guessed he'd been there since we returned from Sacramento, fearing just what our final defeat and his father's disappearance might mean.

I knocked on the door. Coach's voice grew sharper and more menacing. I grabbed the locked doorknob and shook, crying out their names, but no one answered. They were in the back of the house now, in the kitchen, so I ran around the side. I heard a screen door bang, scuffling in the yard, Coach cursing, and Terry screaming.

"Shut up!" Coach roared, silencing her with a blow. "Shut your goddamn mouth!"

I pushed open the side gate and ran into the yard. In the light from an open door I saw Jordi pulling at Coach, who was crouched by the honeysuckle vines over Terry's prone body.

"Stop it!" Jordi cried.

Coach's elbow snapped back in the effort to shake him away. When this didn't work, he turned and shoved his son to the ground.

He was in a fugue state, far outside any shared world. Jordi lunged at him. He managed to pull Coach over onto his hip. I saw Terry's face in dim outline then: rigid, blank, petrified, like an automaton.

Jordi tried to prize his way between the two of them, but Coach's hand found a garden hose stretched at the foot of the back fence. All of a sudden the metal nozzle whipped around and caught Jordi at the ear. His cry pierced the night. He fell onto his shoulder and rolled into a ball, gripping the side of his head with both hands, sobbing uncontrollably. Coach, meanwhile, got up on his knees and resumed his assault of Terry.

I threw myself into the fray, grabbing his raised arm and yanking it with all my might back toward me. My thought was to dislocate his shoulder if I could. But he seemed almost supernaturally strong. He hardly lost his balance. I slammed into him, hoping to knock him off her. But he held his ground this time, too. I felt him rise to his feet under my weight and twist free enough to face me.

The ferocity of his expression, the fact that his skin was smeared black, and the strong smell of gasoline confused me long enough for him to hit me across the face. The pain dizzied my senses, and I fell. At that moment Jordi got up and ran into the house.

Coach turned a third time to Terry. He struck her over and over again. Our resistance only seemed more reason to hurt her. To kill her. I saw no limit to what he might do in that state. "You bitch!" he screamed. "You fucking bitch!"

While I attempted to get to my feet, I sensed more than saw Jordi come back out. I also sensed something odd about the fact that he didn't run at his father right away. He just stood and gaped through his tears.

Then I noticed the outsized knife in his hand, one I remembered seeing before, on his birthday. He was fighting with himself, completely locked in opposing forces, as unable to use that knife as to believe in why he'd brought it out.

"You fucking bitch!"

"Stop it!" Jordi cried again, as if he were trying to shout down Coach's voice in his head. "Stop it! Stop it! Stop it!"

He rushed forward, holding the knife up. I knew he only wanted to hurt his father enough to deflect his anger. He was just looking for the right way to do it. He held the knife sideways as if he meant to slice across the skin, but he couldn't decide how. He turned the point down and jabbed at Coach's shoulder. Coach reared back as the knife slid under his clavicle, cut through the joint, and severed the carotid artery.

It happened so quickly you might not have noticed it. Coach seized up. He turned to face us both and touched the wound with dumbfounded fingers. We watched his shirt and collar darken rapidly with blood. He opened his mouth and tried to speak, but all that came out was an awful gaping.

He fell spasmodically onto the grass. A terrified Jordi dropped to his knees, all his former desperation turned to frantic pleading for his father's life. I tore off my jacket and the flannel shirt I wore underneath, wrapping it around Coach's neck to staunch the blood. I screamed at Jordi to find a phone and call 911, but he couldn't focus enough to think even that far.

Terry had to do it. All at once she sat up and rose to her feet, disappearing into the kitchen. She came out a few seconds later with a cell phone. Over Jordi's anguished sobs I heard her calmly explain that there'd been an accident and they had to send an ambulance right away. Fortunately, one was already in town helping the firefighters at the gym. It took only minutes for paramedics to arrive with the bandages and blood transfusions that would save Coach's life.

The seismic survey, which began on the day we lost the game in Sacramento, was conducted from a ship some fifteen miles off the coast. It was outfitted with a large-scale array of bazooka-shaped airguns fired at short intervals toward the sea floor, discharging over a million pulsed blasts at levels as powerful as dynamite. The noise reverberated hundreds, even thousands of miles, tracking through channels of current, forming beams and shadow zones. It jarred the whole continental shelf, bouncing back ghostly images of seamed mineral deposits in the geological strata.

The gray whales, avoiding the intense sonar activity of the concurrent naval exercise, now ran into yet more perplexing sound fields. Their calls were masked in the ambient interference, and they listened in vain for the navigational echoes they needed. Lost to each other, they began circling aimlessly, their instincts completely confounded. At length they must have just fallen silent.

Isolated strandings were reported in the days that followed. This was not so unusual on the coast. Occasional whales wandered into shallow bays or channels and couldn't get out again, or they were caught in fishing nets that got wound about their flukes. But the number of incidents kept growing, and people started remarking on it. Then, a mass stranding occurred on a beach a few miles north of Fort Bragg. Nineteen gray whales appeared washed up in the surf over the course of a single day. They included several mothers with their calves.

No one knows why collapses like this happen. They seem deliberate, a kind of collective suicide, if such things could be imagined in nature. People began to associate the strandings with the sonar activity because of Suzanne's efforts. There were cautionary warnings against overreaction in the media. The absence of precise causative factors was attested. The essential mystery of biological life was presented as a reason for yet more careful study of the problems that beset marine mammals.

This left people with the feeling that they could only be wrong in their demand for accountability, which was redefined as a need for more of the same science that, by itself, seemed unable to explain things in any morally satisfying way. The good intentions of authorities became all people had to go by, while business went on as usual behind the scenes.

I saw the whales a few days after the gym burned down. The beach receded in a wide sweeping arc to rocks draped with lingering palls of sea spray. Driftwood had collected on the crest at the feet of high dunes. The whales lay hauled up on the sloping beach face as the tide withdrew around them, one after the other unequally spaced into the distance. Most showed cuts and abrasions in their skin that suggested a rough ride to shore. One, the biggest there, had a gash almost a foot deep in its slate-blue hump. There were also bloodstains around its head. This was a clear indication, it seemed to me, of acoustic trauma.

Its eyes, in their concentric folds of wrinkled flesh, were still open. I sat for a long time staring at one of them, waving away the flies. I fancied I saw there the blindness of the whale's world, the slow moving sentience that knew no difference between inside and outside, here and there, only fluctuations of pitch and temperature converted into abstract maps.

I wondered then about the passage from life to death, and if that, too, were less an end than a fluctuation. It seemed reasonable enough to think that death for the whales was not a conclusion to life, not something that happened to them or waited for them. Death came before their birth, before their beginning. It formed the tonic of an existence that was less haunted than haunting. It resonated through all their phrases and passages with a spectral complexity, like a musical idea. I guessed, at any rate, that this was what they listened for in the chord above the frequency or where the overtones fell, even while all harmonics turned to noise and they made their sad yaw in to shore.

I faced the ocean, feeling the stretch in my effort to give a meaning to that eye, which was, in fact, just blank, sense-less, sealed up in dumb necessity. That's all I really had to go by: the event of the songs vanishing, of the spectral sounds deserting them, when the whales gave in finally to inertia. Still, I didn't think I was entirely off-base. Maybe that giving in lasted as long as it took cutting out at the limits of pain, or maybe it lasted through all the minutes, hours, or days of their final drift. Either way, it hinted at an underlying pull toward fatality that was also, strangely, a principle of life, a deep precariousness in every equilibrium struck in nature.

It would take me a long time to put things together in this way, but I did at least have the feeling then that I would need to understand, and that it would take all my resources and skill to understand, the question that was enigmatically addressing me on that beach, in wave, in sand, in windrows of foam, in the scattered combs of by-the-wind sailors, in one small cloud slowly vanishing from the blue sky. The effort, indeed, would knot my heart up in strange obsessions and scruples for years to come. It would drive me along in my mistakes as well as in a sense of purpose. Maybe it wasn't so surprising either. Maybe the sense of purpose was only ever a mistake, an uncertain movement in the dark, and that was our nature, was nature in us. If so, it seemed to me that what we had to do was feel that nature in ourselves more honestly; we had to listen as well as see and know in the other relation to death it implied, like a whale in the perfect streamlines of its dive. At least that would be my aim from then on.

"ONCE!" CRIED RYDER, watching his shot fall cleanly through the net. He let his hand float above his head a moment. He let it linger with the pleasure of revolving things, the semi-eclipsed planets we made of our impulses, the orbits drawn in infinite space.

It was a bright summer day at the middle school. I'd chanced on him shooting around like this on a visit to Mendocino about ten years after I graduated from high school. It was the first time we'd seen each other in a long while. I hadn't been back much after my mother died. The memory of her last years was too painful. The two of us had continued to live by Point Cabrillo, and I ran the kennel pretty much on my own for several years. She quit smoking, but whatever gain there was in that came with a corresponding loss of spirit. Emphysema is a dwindling disease. Well before the end my mother was little more than a wraith. She lived between her bed and a chair, attached by a catheter to an oxygen tank and addicted to the morphine the doctors put her on. She'd spend hours staring out a window listening to the wheeze of her shallow breath, her mind a blank.

When I was twenty-four she contracted pneumonia. We both knew there would be no recovering from it. She claimed it was a relief to her. The days before she died were the happiest she'd known in a long time. She seemed to be herself again, talking in clear sentences and even laughing. She said death was easy, "like walking from one room into another." I was the only one crying when she walked into that other room, nodding off to sleep one day in a Fort Bragg hospital bed.

I passed the ball back to Ryder, and he dribbled around the perimeter, thinking, What now? What next? What follows what? Maybe I won't shoot it. Maybe I'll keep it. *His eyes narrowed provocatively on the prospect. Then he flowed into a hook shot from a good fifteen feet away. The ball banged off the backboard and in.*

"Twice!" he hissed, like a snake.

His hand drifted up his shirtless torso to graze the kinky hair on his chest. He was laughing, easy. The voices in his head seemed to have left him alone for the day. Their hiatus filled the sun-shot air with a feeling of reprieve.

He took the ball and backed into a corner, drawing the angle to the basket as acute as he could make it, preparing for the next shot.

A flock of blackbirds came into view over the playground. Ryder promptly forgot what he was doing, straightened up with the ball crooked under one arm, and observed them move together against the blue sky, like a shape-shifting spirit. Not one of them made a wrong move. Not one of them was out of place.

I observed them, too, thinking of maneuver waves and reaction times too rapid for individual choice to be involved. That sort of precision was becoming the rule with me. A year or so before my mother passed away, her parents began to show more of an interest in us. I think they felt bad about how distant they'd been my whole life. I'd already started taking classes at the community college in Fort Bragg, and they generously offered to pay my way at Sonoma State, where I enrolled the fall after my mother died.

I took my studies seriously, wanting to make good on their investment. I graduated with honors in biology and the support of my professors, who helped me get into the PhD program in environmental science at UC Santa Cruz. For the next several years I'd be engrossed in various research projects, learning new modes of thinking and new expectations for myself. It wasn't easy. I was thrown in with people who had a lot of confidence in themselves. But as Chase's dad had said, I had a feeling for systems, for the principle of least energy governing a cell, an organism, or an ecological niche.

I also had a good grasp of why scientists call most systems "history dependent." If you press into a pillow, it will yield to your touch, but when you release your hand, the pillow won't spring back exactly to its original state. A piece of iron placed in a magnetic field stays magnetized after it's taken out of the field. It will carry the memory of the applied force into the present as a kind of lag. They call this hysteresis. It plays a crucial role, for instance, in the process of cell division, which is to say in life itself.

Things hadn't been easy for me in other ways. What I was good at made me more of a taciturn man than I wanted to be. It was hard to trust myself. But I liked to think I was working on that. I was also a patient man, and I think pretty open and curious. I may have felt especially optimistic at the time, since I'd connected with Suzanne after having lost touch with her many years before. She'd just moved from San Francisco to Santa Cruz to begin an undergraduate degree in, of all things, oceanography.

We'd begun spending a lot of time together. That was one reason for my visit to Mendocino: she and I had come to visit her mother in their house on Little Lake Road. I still wasn't sure exactly what kind of relationship the two of us were going to have, but I had good reason to expect things would go well enough for me this time around, now that I'd caught up with myself a little more.

I'd also come to see Fox and Zach. Both were still there. Fox had taken on most of the responsibility for his dad's ranch. Zach was involved in some shady business that involved him ferrying carloads of marijuana trim over the Oregon border, where it was purged into a drug called shatter. We'd met for beers at the Caspar Inn the night before and reminisced about old times. I eagerly listened for news about the others. I'd lost touch with them as well.

Coach spent a year in prison after recovering from his injury, and after that he moved with his family to Eureka, where he still lived. He was squarely on the wagon again. Jordi had moved to Texas, where his mom also ended up. He was married and working as a home mortgage broker. Coop split his time between Portland and Alaska, where he made his money as a fisherman during the summer salmon season. He was as much a loner as ever, but doing all right in his fashion. Sky ended up going to school at Chico State and now lived in Tahoe. Fox heard she'd married a doctor and was raising a family.

Neither asked about Chase, so I didn't tell them what I knew: that after playing basketball at Stanford, where he helped lead their team to a national championship, he'd moved to New York and become a bond trader on Wall Street. Suzanne had found that out looking it up online. No one had ever heard from him again after high school.

Ryder snapped out of his reverie and shot the ball. It grazed the edge of the backboard and bounced around the rim one, two, three times before deciding to drop.

"Thrice!"

On his next turn he came in to the basket, glancing at me over his shoulder, inviting contact. I waved my arms as he dipped around and under the hoop for a reverse lay-up. These shots were a specialty of his. They required degrees of spin so complex it seemed as if the ball was magnetized.

I suggested we play a game of one-on-one. Ryder agreed, but first he had to fix his shoe, a black sneaker with a hole under the ball of his foot. He walked over to the ice plant and sat on the curb, producing from his pocket a small piece of cardboard. He fit it into the shoe over the hole.

To make sure he got it right, he put on his glasses. One tine was lashed to the frame with dental floss. At length he slipped his foot back into the shoe and stood, making sure the cardboard stayed in place. I looked on, bemused. He was in enough of a good mood to warrant a little prying into his still enigmatic past.

"Where'd you grow up, Ryder?"

Walking on that shoe he said, "Around and around."

"How old are you?"

"Old as the hills," he said, more pointedly. I could tell he wasn't going to bite. He probably never would. He didn't like too much history.

We started the game, nice and slow, no pressure to do more than embody imaginary foes for a while. Ryder wasn't so fond of facing you up or playing directly with your center of gravity like that. His kind of dueling was more elliptical. He showed you his back and looked for ways to fool you.

He forced me to push a little to keep him out of the key. I pressed against him, feeling his bony hip against my stomach and chest. When he made off in one direction, I knew he was already going in another. I smelled, along with a faint odor of ditchwater, the joint he must have smoked before I got there. The world might have been even loopier for him than I thought. He uncoiled from the knees up and stretched into a jump shot. I whacked his arm.

"Foul!"

We started again. He backed into the post and I eased him out of the key, my white hands on his black skin. Our shoes scraped together on the rough concrete. Suddenly we disengaged. In the interval formed between us, I saw his shoulders twitching, his head bobbing. I had him where he didn't want to be, but he had me in the right state of uncertainty. He faked up, I jumped, and he was gone, moving fluidly in to the basket for a layup.

"You must have been the star of your team when you were in high school, Ryder."

He laughed, trotting around to the top of the key. Not for the first time I had a feeling there were lots of things in this world I still had to learn. "One of many," he told me. "One of many." Then he held out his hands for the ball.

About the Author

STEFAN MATTESSICH is the author of three other novels: *East Brother*, a satire of gentrification in a California beach town; *The Riverbed*, about imaginative teenagers coming to learn about the darker sides of the suburban fantasy they call home; and *A Precarious Man*, about the search for love and belonging in neoliberal times. He went to Yale College and has a PhD in literature from the University of California, Santa Cruz, where he wrote a monograph on the fiction of Thomas Pynchon entitled *Lines of Flight*, published by Duke University Press. He teaches English at Santa Monica College and lives in Los Angeles.